The Princess Gardener

The Princess Gardener

Michael Strelow

Winchester, UK
Washington, USA

First published by Our Street Books, 2018
Our Street Books is an imprint of John Hunt Publishing Ltd., Laurel House, Station Approach,
Alresford, Hants, SO24 9JH, UK
office1@jhpbooks.net
www.johnhuntpublishing.com
www.ourstreet-books.com

For distributor details and how to order please visit the 'Ordering' section on our website.

ISBN: 978 1 78535 674 2
978 1 78535 675 9 (ebook)
Library of Congress Control Number: 2017937406

A CIP catalogue record for this book is available from the British Library.

Design: Stuart Davies

Printed and bound by CPI Group (UK) Ltd, Croydon, CR0 4YY, UK

For Ava, Audrey, Lewis, Jackson, Zephyr,
my best critics and marvelous creatures every one.

Acknowledgements

Without the critical eye of Audrey G., this book would never have seen the light. Her sharp questions and critical eye kept me rethinking and trying to make this a better book. I hope the result pleases her, those listed in the dedication, and maybe a few more.

Chapter One

What do you expect? I was only five years old the first time I said it, so no one paid much attention. But as I grew older, I said it more and more and more until they knew they would have to forbid it. I said, "I would rather be a gardener than a princess."

In the princess business, this is kind of like admitting to being crazy or something. "Gardener? Why would you want to be a gardener when you're already a princess? Gardeners' little daughters all want to be a princess, Eugenie. Have you lost your mind?"

And this went on for a long time until I learned to tone down my request and just take my gardening chances when I could get them.

For as long as I could remember I had liked digging in the dirt and planting flowers and vegetables. And especially trees. My mother and father would leave me with the nanny and the gardeners of the castle, and all afternoon I could get as dirty as I wanted. I could smell the earth, and make things grow. One whole afternoon I spent following a snail to see where it was going, my nose close behind it across the fragrant ground, the sunlight flickering with shadows. The gardener laughed because he saw what I was doing. I pulled back my dark princess hair with one hand so it wouldn't fall in my eyes, and eye to eye with the snail—a big brown beauty—I shuffled my way in the shadows and, finally, into a crack in the rock garden. "Ah," I said. "That was nice. Thank you, Betty." That's what I had named my big brown beauty snail.

And she was the just the beginning of my collection.

"What's that you've got behind your back, Eugenie?" my mother asked.

"Oh nothing. I was just going to...going to look for a small box. Or something," I replied. The castle smelled of the big fires kept going in the many fireplaces. "Maybe some kind of cage?"

"Eugenie! Let me see what you have," my mother insisted, so I held out my hand and showed the five potato bugs curled up in one hand. I kept the other hand behind my back.

"Take those outside immediately. No, wait. What's in the other hand?"

I tried the trick where you put both hands behind you and then switch the contents and come out with the same thing. But it didn't work.

"No, both hands out. What have you got in the other one?"

Well, it was worms. A whole handful of worms that I knew would get me into trouble. I had brought them in to see what would happen if they got warmer, but I got a storm instead.

"Eugenie, take both...*all* of those outside where they belong. And then come back here. We should talk about some things. It's time to leave some things behind and begin others."

I knew all this was coming. I had known it for a long time now. Recently I had been asked to dress up for dinner. Way up! Pearls, those shiny shoes that hurt, the tight dress I couldn't loosen even when I ate too much. And my hair! The maids pulled and tugged it too tight to make some kind of knot behind, a knot that was fashionable at court but hurt a kid's hair. There I was wanting bugs and worms and being tucked and coiffed into misery.

The palace fires burned, and people went here and there being important. But I couldn't wait to get into the dirt. I had my digging clothes all ready near the small door that went out into the garden. They had been exiled there on wooden hooks since my mother found them hanging in my very large closet with all the princess gear. My overalls and shirt, given to me as a birthday present by the gardener, were now growing too small. When he gave them to me, I had no problem getting outside. But now, well, more and more princess duties were piling up, and I spent way too much time sitting in velvet chairs and not near enough smelling the earth.

Planting trees was fun because I was allowed to dig a deep hole and then dump in some water and some dirt, then the tree, its root ball all wrapped up like a big present. Then I'd fill in with dirt and compost and right at the end, cut the strings that held the burlap in place. It felt like I was unwrapping a present for the world. Then, with the gardener's help, more water and finally more dirt. At the end of it all, I was gloriously dirty from top to bottom. I felt at home, I felt just like the tree sticking out of the earth into the sky, I felt lovely. The tree poked up to the sky where it would be headed for years. I poked down into the fine dirt. My hands and knees, I felt, were like special dirt badges. I held up my hands for the gardener to see. And he held up his to show me.

The nanny, Corrine, was there to see that I didn't hurt myself, and she, like my mother, didn't approve of all that dirt. Corrine wore a fresh white dress, and I would chase her around with my dirty hands pretending to want to paint big dirty handprints on that clean canvas. She'd scream, "NO, NO, NO, Eugenie," and scurry away, and the gardener and I would laugh until we fell down. He showed me how to wipe my hands on the wet grass to get them clean, leaving my dirt signature as royal as any I ever could make.

But as I grew older, I had to beg and beg to be allowed to

work with the gardeners. I made deals with mother. If she allowed me "dirt time," then I would, without complaint, learn the princess ways that mother and father insisted on—tea party behavior, how to greet dignitaries from other countries, how to curtsey and stand and sit and even turn my head. Fake smiles and how-do-you-dos. Keep my nose pointed evenly out into space while accepting compliments. Tilt my head back slightly to laugh a little; cover my mouth to laugh a lot.

There was a right way, it turned out, and a wrong way to do all these things, and a princess had to be a model for the rest of the country. Alas, in no case did any of these duties involve getting my hands deliciously wet and dirty, in plunging them into warm soil on a spring day, or mixing manure and dirt and leaves into a compost pile. And, also, alas, none of the princess duties involved that feeling I got when I saw the flowers I had planted pop from their stems, and shout colors of glory across the whole garden: marigolds, long-stemmed daisies, dahlias with flowers as big as my head.

And there were row after row of blueberries mulched with apricot-colored sawdust like a dream of the moon. I learned the most important things in life from the gardeners: the nitrogen stuff and the manure stuff and the water-saving stuff, the way plants love mulch, yes. But also the way a thirsty plant would curl its leaves to save water, the yellow signs that a plant was not getting enough food, the sad droop of a plant that was not happy where it was and needed less sun or more sun or some other tending.

All this was kind of like learning to read, and I loved the reading, learning the new garden language. I thought of it as learning to read plant. My parents wanted me to begin three useful foreign languages that would be valuable for diplomatic purposes later. But I learned to speak fluent plant first. Plants would tell me when they were happy by glowing and reaching for the sun. They'd complain about lack of food or water or crowding.

While putting on a beautiful dress because I had to appear to greet guests before an important dinner that evening, I dreamed of dirt and trimming roses and tying up the espaliered apple trees. When my attendants asked me if I would like these earrings or those, this belt or that, I'd say, "What? Oh, I don't know. Either one. It doesn't matter. How about one of each?" My attendants looked at each other knowingly as if they had just witnessed the beginning of the end for the whole kingdom. The princess loses her mind, and all is lost! You can't imagine how crabby that made them, as if I were spitting on everything they thought important.

Again, I learned quickly to turn down my dislike for princess trappings. A little bit anyway. And it became more and more clear to the servants that none of the princess business mattered to me. I was not interested in everything that they were absolutely sure I should be interested in. I even overheard one call me an "ungrateful snot." And I immediately thought of the snail's beautiful trail glistening across the fine, brown dirt. And I smiled and accepted the name: I was The Snot. I'd try to work out this princess business though, because I had to. No real choice in the matter.

And this trade-off might have been satisfactory for everyone, but each day—I was ten now, almost eleven—I was expected to leave my love of dirt and turn to the family business of being an example for the rest of the country. When we rode in carriages, I would look out the window at the kids working with their families in the fields and in the big gardens they tended. And I would sigh a most un-princess-like sigh, though I had been told repeatedly not to, that sighing was a sign of a "disorganized mind, and untidy soul." I looked up these words and said to myself, "Yes I am both disorganized and untidy." Unless there was dirt involved. I was, of course, not allowed to add that part because to say so would be bad mannered and insolent. Sassiness did not, I was informed, become a princess.

And yet I sighed. I couldn't help my sigh of longing after the dirt. And I pined for the dirt just as the young girls in the countryside, I was told, pined to be the princess. It didn't matter. I would have changed places with any one of them in a heartbeat. The Sighing Snot, I thought. That's what I'm becoming. I wondered if I could write that in the grass with my muddy hands.

One day in the village when my family was making an appearance to unify the people behind a new law, I spotted across the crowd of heads a girl about my age dressed in farming clothes. I had been grumbling to myself about the dress I had to wear, my shoes pinched and people kept telling me what to do and where to stand. I wanted her comfortable shoes, the way she tucked her hair back—all that comfort. I pictured myself in her place. She could have mine. I smiled and waved to the crowd. Then we went on to the local school.

"Princess Eugenie, dear, be sure to greet the teachers first and then nod to the children," said Corrine, who had now been promoted to "Protocol Mistress" from being the nanny who feared my dirty handprints. "They will be lined up to your left and then pass in front..." And there I glazed over, I think. All I heard was blah blah blah though I could see her mouth still moving. I thought of the whole business as a dance. Left foot. Right foot. Spin and twirl. "...and then the guard will escort you to the..." Blah. Blah.

The schoolroom was bright and cheery and had benches and tables and things for writing. It smelled like one of the tool rooms in the stable, maybe because of the wood stacked near the fireplace and the fresh leather door hinges. I supposed I was the first princess ever in the room, and that probably accounted for the many vases of wildflowers placed around. As I looked, I thought that everything I really needed was here: a roof, some friends, a fire, a teacher. And then I would have my own garden. And maybe a cow.

I said, "I greet you in the name of the King and Queen who send their wishes for prosperity and good fortune. I am Princess Eugenie, daughter of...." And I launched into my pedigree, the names of a few notable ancestors, and the mention of not one, but two famous battles that resulted in the formation of our kingdom. "...and Courtenleigh, and Brodens," I finished.

The children were hushed for the beginning, but I had said all this so many times that it seemed to me like one long word coming out of my mouth, though it took more than two minutes. I saw that the littlest children had begun to fidget, and I really wanted to break into some silly song, maybe a dance too, and entertain the most fidgety among them. But I didn't. This was serious: and it was tradition and custom and convention and ritual—all the things that held a nation together. I could hear the echo of my father's voice in my own; hear the song of my sober-faced ancestors ringing in the modest rafters of the schoolhouse.

One small child burst out, "I can't seeee!" And there followed an adult chorus of hushes like a high wind through the trees. I saw him peeking around bigger children, and I stepped forward and spoke to him.

"Hello there. What's your name?"

He stood stock still, eyes wide. Maybe the princess was a dragon who now would belch fire and fry him to a crisp. The other children moved away from him leaving the poor little guy rooted on the spot and waiting for the fire. No name came out of his mouth. He had stopped breathing. I touched his shoulder to bring him back to life, and he gasped. Finally, breathing in and out, he blurted out, "Orlando!" as if he had said all there was to be said in the whole world, one word that took in the stars and moon and storms on all the oceans.

And then another voice, one I would come to know and love, but at this time was a sort of a raspy note full of itself. "His name is Orlando and he's the youngest. That's why he's afraid. "

"And you are?"

"Jake. That's with a J, your highness-est. I'm eight." I had met Jake, and someone put a gentle hand on Jake's shoulder, maybe to keep him from speaking further.

And then there she was. She was my height, had the same color hair but a little longer, and—this was the amazing part—had a perfect copy of my face! I couldn't believe it. I just stared and stared at her. I couldn't believe nobody else saw it. She was me—more tanned, hair different. But me! Our noses, eyebrows, cheekbones, and chins. Our lips and earlobes! How could that be? She paused with her hand on Jake and Jake, like a spooky horse, became quiet and stared at me, gentled by his sister.

"That's my sister, Alyssa," Jake added. She's eleven."

I read somewhere that everyone had a doppelganger—a pretty good copy of yourself—just waiting out there to be discovered. Most people went their whole lives without seeing their double. I just found mine. But somehow my clothes and my entourage had become my perfect disguise.

And then she looked at me looking at her. And she saw what I saw. We locked eyes, and then she looked away, pretended to be fiddling with something or other; then she smoothed her dress. But we both knew.

"I'm pleased," I said slowly, to put the children at ease, "to meet you all, Orlando, Jake," and here I looked directly at my double in disguise, "and all the rest of you. I hope to see you all again." Here came both my eyebrows raised as the only way to talk to her right now, she who was me. "And please take my good wishes to your mothers and fathers. Study well with your teachers and give them the respect they certainly deserve. They work in your best interest to build a better..." And then I heard myself going blah, blah, blah again.

I had to wade through the rest of the official visit, make the best of it. But as soon as the school visit was over, I begged my mother to let me go again to the village schools to make more visits and encourage the children and teachers on behalf of the royal family. I said this time I would take small gifts and begin my own my career as goodwill ambassador to the people. I wanted to do it alone, to start small. And, mother, I argued, "Visiting more schools close by would be a great practice for more important duties later. But I don't know..."

You know how that arguing goes. Make your best case, wait a while, watch your mother's eyes. Then, oh yes, add one more thing when you think you've got a chance. "Mother, just think how proud the King will be if I do it on my own." Done. Sealed. She insisted though that the guardian retinue go with me, and I accepted the conditions. I knew I would have company of some sort. But once there, I'd get out alone and look for my double.

I scheduled Alyssa's school for the second one I visited. I spotted her in the back row, the same girl, my face. I was, of course, "all princessed up," so between my swept up hair, the pearl necklace and the brilliant dress of white silk and pink ribbons, I didn't look quite like Alyssa there in the back row. Not to the other children, at least. Not to my retinue. But Alyssa knew right away what was going on. I passed among the children, and we smiled at each other. Then came Alyssa, and it was like smiling into a mirror.

We both wanted to sit down and talk to that other-me right away. Who wouldn't? Imagine seeing yourself there like a big you-doll dressed up like a farmer or a princess. I wanted to set out tea and cookies and spend the afternoon asking her questions and laughing. I wanted to clear out the whole world so just the two of us could talk and go for a walk where she would show me her garden and fields and take me into the barn with its horse and leather smell and the sweet hay.

But, of course, that would be impossible just then. My official people kept me moving through this school. There were five more schools to visit this afternoon, and the schedule was very tight. But we both knew we would talk somehow, someplace. And talk and talk and talk, it turned out. And even some more of what I wanted from the first time I set eyes on her: time to talk, garden time, time to breathe.

I knew I would have to make the first move because Alyssa could never get into the palace without an invitation. She and her family would be welcome in the great courtyard on special days of celebration, of course. She could come as near to me as a cheer for the royal family, the "long live the King" part. Alyssa's mother and father were farmers, the best farmers around since they worked hard to take care of the land and raised fine crops. My mother and father always told me how important the farmers were, how everything we ate came from them, and everything we did at the castle should keep their health and valuable work in mind. But I couldn't just point out Alyssa and have her come visit me. That would certainly call attention to our double-ness. I would have to plan this carefully. And that was how I got to meet Alyssa.

At the castle after the long visits to schools, I began my plan. My visits were grand successes, it turned out. Lots of great publicity. The village was abuzz. I mentioned to mother that I had seen some beautiful farms while traveling between schools. Could I maybe (there's my key word, *maybe*; it always works nicely in starting out an argument) visit the best farms in order to give out some awards for the most successful farming techniques?

"You always said the farmers were the most important part of the kingdom, didn't you?" I pleaded. "And it would make them feel like we really appreciated the work they did." And I listed off the cows, pigs, turnips, beans, wheat, cheese, chickens, geese—and took a deep breath and ticked off the rest on my fingers.

My mother quickly said, "Yes, yes, that sounds like a fine idea. I'm sure the King..." And I knew it would work. My best advice about arguing is to have some kind of list and to use it as soon as possible. That and the maybes.

The visits would be such good practice for when I had to do that kind of thing later, more serious kinds of awards. And with words and lists I painted a picture for her how I would spread good will among the farmers and remind them that they were the life-blood of the whole realm. Without them no one would eat. They were doing the most important work, and everyone appreciated them. And so on and so on until mother began nodding that good ideas came in all kinds of packages and these farm visits might be good policy and the schools had worked out.

Finally, she seemed to come around so far that she talked about the whole business as her own idea. She said we'd see what the King said. But I knew she was the one really making the decision. The whole, "I'll have to ask the King" thing was just smoke and mirrors, just pretending so the whole kingdom seemed to be in order from the King on down to the least citizen. High to low, order made order, my father pronounced often.

I thought I might even push mother just a little farther, so I suggested that I might dress in farm clothes to, you know, help make the farmers feel comfortable. Mother grew silent and pictured her daughter out in public dressed for working the soil, and she began shaking her head and said, "No, that would be a bad idea." It would give a wrong impression (the whole kingdom ran on giving the right impressions!) and would not be suitable. "No, not suitable at all, I think." And she looked me up and down as if trying to imagine me dressed to work the fields, not just work in the garden. She always thought of my gardening as left over play from when I was little, and she thought that like other kinds of play, it would have to slowly cease as I got older. Duty would call; I would answer. The proper order of things. My silk dresses on one end, Alyssa's homespun dresses on the other end.

When the Queen presented the idea of farm visits to the King, he was against it. Unsafe. Untidy. Unseemly. Unhealthy. Unpolitic, and un—something else and then something else too. I overheard through a very thick door and the "uns" went on for a long time. But the Queen knew that if she made the case to the King, and slowly presented all the advantages I had outlined that he would allow it. And, after the proper amount of snorting and huffing, he did.

The Queen felt right. Of course, I felt delighted. I don't know how the King felt, but my mother reported that "your father was certainly pleased" that he had done the right thing for me and for the kingdom.

One thing to be clear: there was to be no compromise of the clothes I would wear—princess clothes only. OK, so maybe not the big state-occasion clothes with the pearls and tiara, but the nice stuff, anyway. I was to look assertively royal. I could live with that. I'd *have* to live with that. I knew to pick my battles. Win the winables that was my motto. The clothes would be princess clothes. But I also knew how to compress and pack a set of gardening clothes into a small bag that I would hide in the carriage well before the visit just in case I could think of a way to wear them. Spoil my dress by falling in a puddle? Lean over and have a cow take a bite out of my skirt? Well, I'd think about it. There might be a way to get the farming clothes on. But if not, it felt good to have a second plan there hidden in the carriage.

The day before my visit, it rained all across the kingdom. The farmers were joyful; the crops were getting dry. The palace was busy closing windows and rearranging the gravel that had been disheveled by the rain. As a secret gardener I always immediately felt joy when it rained. I guess I was thinking like a plant and how plants would stretch and turn their faces to the rain, stretch their roots down into damp soil. Rain made everything seem freshly scrubbed and new. I loved it because plants loved it.

I really liked to walk in the gardens just to smell the rain, the dirt, and listen to how delighted the birds seemed after a rain. Everything woke up, it seemed. The things that couldn't have been sleeping also woke: rocks and sticks and the sun. Not only was the world awake while it rained, but it sang. The singing wasn't coming into my ears. It came in smells and sounds: warm wet dirt, clicks and splats of trees shaking the rain drops around with their leaves. And there was the girl at the school who, like two plants growing side by side, had grown my exact princess-face while living on a farm not far from the castle. Tomorrow couldn't come soon enough.

Chapter Two

The rain had stopped during the night and the morning sported polished pearls everywhere the sun touched. I smiled to myself when I thought of the package of clothes hidden away in the carriage. Something about hidden things in general made me smile: the roots of plants, the clothes in the carriage, the gardener secreted away inside the princess.

We arrived at Alyssa's parents' farm just as the roads were drying, but here and there a puddle glistened and, frankly, puddles still called to me to splash and romp.

I got out of the carriage holding my dress high and peering around for Alyssa.

"Your Majesty, welcome to our farm," spoke Alyssa's father with just a little bit of quiver in his voice. I could tell he had been practicing it, and now saying it out loud seemed to relieve his nervousness.

"I'm a mere princess," I answered. "So just princess is enough." I laughed. "Mother is 'Your Majesty' around our house." I turned to his wife. "I think all mothers should be addressed as Your Majesty, don't you?"

She blushed and then quickly laughed and said, "I'll have to work on that with my husband and children. I should have them trained in no time." I liked her immediately.

Alyssa's father took a deep breath and continued with what he had memorized. "Princess, if you'll follow me this way, I can show you whatever parts of our humble farm that would please you." He proudly led us across the tidy yard toward a field just popping with bright green shoots. I think he wanted us to see what his hard work had created. I nodded in agreement at the fence. We stood together admiring the field in silence.

"I would especially like to see the garden part of your farm, too. And your barn, of course." I could see the inside of the barn was neat as a pin, and it would be inconsiderate of me not to recognize all his housekeeping there.

There was no dust, and the floors were swept, the animals washed, the rows of harnesses and reins oiled and gleaming. There was order everywhere in this disorderly business of animals and crops and things that broke and had to be mended. I knew that all this was specially arranged for my visit, and I looked around for something real, something that was more like muddy hands and knees when I worked in the garden. And I quickly found it.

There peering through a crack in the stall boards was a small muddy face with big eyes like a large cat with stringy hair. Then it disappeared. There it is again. I glanced around to try to catch where it would appear again. It was like trying to guess where a fairy would show up or an elf or a... There, there it is again.

"That's my little brother, Princess." Alyssa appeared at my side. She had seen me trying to follow the flitting face around the barn. "He's a gentle and wonderful soul, actually. But he likes to have fun. You met at the school, I think. He not shy, really." And then Alyssa leaned over to whisper, "My parents think he's up playing in his room where he was told to stay during your visit. I think his curiosity got the best of him."

I paused the tour by holding up my hand. Everyone waited quietly while I turned to Alyssa. Frankly, I was wondering when everyone would notice that she and I had the same face and hair color, but everyone apparently was so occupied by royal paraphernalia that no one was doing comparisons.

The pause went on. So I spoke. "I would like to speak to this young woman alone, please. We would like to sit down somewhere in the shade and have tea. Would that be too much trouble?" It was exactly what I had been planning for, Alyssa and me, tea, laughing by ourselves. I held my breath to see if it would happen just as I wanted. I was willing to have the crowd of my people and her family off mingling somewhere. This would be close enough to perfect.

There was scurrying about. My people worked with Alyssa's father and mother to find a table and two chairs all arranged under an enormous apple tree that seemed to fill the sky near the house. There were apples so high up that I wondered out loud how anyone would pick those.

Alyssa, laughed and pointed to the highest spot in the huge tree. "We have our own special tool for getting those down when they are ripe." She looked around and spotted Jake again, this time up on a shed that leaned against the barn. "There's the tool." She laughed. "Jake is more at home climbing trees than he is on the ground. In the fall, he seems to fly up the tree and then he tosses down apples into a blanket we hold as a target below. My mother used to be afraid that he'd fall. But he never even slips, and now Mother never even worries about it. We think he might be part bird, part squirrel. My father jokes that my mother was scared by woodland critters when she was pregnant with him. And he has their powers now."

Alyssa was joyous telling about her scamp of a brother, and quickly it seemed we had been talking all our lives.

The tea came out hot. We sat in the shade while my retinue made the silly lines they always seemed to be making, and Alyssa's father and mother continually offered them places to sit: the bench on the porch, the shady windbreak near the house, the arbor of hops they kept for making household remedies.

Nearly every house in the country had some kind of

herb garden kept for making healing teas and specifics for colds and coughs. Everyone grew a hops plant or two stretching over a porch or pinned up to a stout wooden arbor.

The whole world then disappeared as Alyssa and I talked and talked surrounded by healing plants, the occasional moo from the barn, and our lookout, Jake, from his perch near the peak of the barn roof making sure we were safe. He reminded me of the gargoyles carved into the corners of the stone castle walls, woodland imps with popping eyes that warded off evil spirits or something. I was never sure what the castle creatures were for, so Jake, crouching on the roof, was not a problem for me either. Our gargoyle disappeared and then appeared again, this time in a beech tree that shaded the house. Alyssa told me that you just had to ignore him after a while. He went his own way and really was a good small person. We laughed like sisters. We exchanged how marvelous it seemed that we could sit here together drinking tea.

I said, "They don't seem to notice, do they? I mean, are we the only ones who see it?"

She lowered her voice like a conspirator. "I know!" and then like the punch line to a joke she added, "I think my freckles and your not-freckles must keep them from seeing what we see. If I stay out of the sun, my freckles grow very light, like in the winter. Then the sun brings them back again in summer. I'm guessing that freckles are the best disguise."

I began thinking immediately that we could manage the freckles. I didn't know how Alyssa would feel about it, but we had so little time that I had to get it out. I proposed that we start working toward the day that we might be able to switch places—or at least give a try. Just for a little while? I thought she would be perfectly sane to say no. A farm girl caught trying to be the princess? Who knew what kind of trouble that would bring?

"If somebody finds us out, well, we can just say it was a girl-joke and no harm done. Can't we? And that it was my idea all the way." I looked at her quizzically. "But it would be very exciting if we could do it." I thought this would be the hard part. Would the whole idea of "exciting" be enough for her to take the risks?

Alyssa rubbed her chin. "Nobody would punish *you*, of course. And my parents would get over it pretty quick. But what about all those people?" She pointed at my guards and the assorted palace folk I had dragged along. "Wouldn't they have some laws against it or something? Would they throw me into a dungeon," and here's where I knew we were going to be able to do this swap. She continued, "...and leave my poor mother weeping at the gate with a bowl of fresh fruit for me?" Alyssa thought the image very funny, and it was then that I was sure she would be a great and secret friend for this whole business. Alyssa added looking around, "How can they not see what we see? Freckles and clothes. If that's enough, I'm sure we'll have no problems." And we both laughed at the perfect disguises in her homespun dress and my silk and brocade with tiny gold threads. Freckles were like frosting on the cake. We could do this.

"Or maybe they can't imagine that a princess and a farm girl would look exactly alike." I raised my eyebrows like I'd been practicing to show amazement. Alyssa curled up her hair on her neck to about the length of mine, just for a second, and then let it drop again.

And then she made a joke. "Do you think they saw it then?" And we both laughed as if the whole world—their world, anyway—was outside our private joke. And it was. Alyssa's voice was the same as mine. She had the same silly laugh. She threw her head back the same way. We began plotting seriously.

We talked until the gaggle of adults seemed to get a little restless. I'd need some sun tan, some freckles, of course. She'd need to work on her nails. Haircuts, eyebrows, some work on walks. Could we do it? For how long? And this was the other side of our scheme. Would everyone think as we did that it was a capital joke if we got caught. The voices of my mother and father rang in my head: things in order, things as they should be and always were. Order is safety and harmony and certainty.

We would see if we could change places for some length of time—a week? A month? Half a year? More? But we would have to know much more about the other's life first to pull off the exchange.

We would write back and forth, and the letters would be carried by special couriers that I would arrange. No one else would read the letters. We could write anything, but details would be important: servants' names, brother's name, parents' habits, royal duties, ways to be around servants, ways to be around friends, how to go to school, how to treat tutors that came to the castle. And many more things too.

We agreed that we would write and write and write until we thought we could be each other, act out another life, pretend without a hitch. And then we would do the swap. At first one week. And then we'd meet and talk about what was easy, what was hard. It was settled. I would send the special courier soon with the first letter.

School! I thought. That would be wonderful. Not by myself in a big echoing room with one scowling tutor's face with words coming out of it. School with real children and silliness and everyone with different shoes. I imagined the shoes for some reason, the flicker of different shoes like butterflies across the wooden schoolroom floor. And the happy chatter afterward of children running noisily free after sitting too long. I imagined a kind of life I had only seen at a distance before and now found myself thirsty for it.

"Alyssa. Do you think this will work? I've wanted to get out of that castle for as long as I can remember. I remember looking out the window, and as far as I could see there was something better, I thought. Whenever we passed through a village in our carriage, I wanted to jump out and run in a glorious pack with the children. Even if we could just do it for a little while, what a great adventure it would be for me."

"We can. I'm sure we can," Alyssa replied. "There are so many things I haven't seen and done, too. I would look toward the castle and wonder and wonder. I have no idea what goes on in there."

"Oh, I'll tell you everything you need to know. It's not that hard, really. When to do this, when that. Mostly the kind of stuff to make you wish you were back here."

We laughed so hard at the idea of switching lives that I'm sure the echoes off the barn wall sounded like the same laugh twice, and then the echo on top. For a second, our laughs were one thing, and the two of us were one thing.

Finally, when we could talk again, Alyssa said, "This princess business is as interesting to me as you say the farm business is to you. Maybe just because it's new and exciting. I have never worn anything made of silk, though I've seen it. It made me want to touch it just to find out if it's as smooth as it looks."

I held out the hem of my dress for her to touch. She laughed and said it felt like it was alive, so smooth and slippery. And we both got to laughing again. Then silly set in and we couldn't talk any more, it seemed, without breaking into giggles.

The restless adults began discussing the time, the weather, the schedule, the afternoon plans. My farm clothes hidden in the carriage would stay hidden until another day. We all said a formal goodbye. Alyssa winked. That was how it began. Everything was in motion, a motion so different from yesterday that it hung deliciously everywhere like sweet flavored air. I had only to breathe it in.

I sent the courier; Alyssa wrote right back. The letters started short but got longer and longer very quickly. Each detail we revealed about our lives reminded us of other details we would have to give. Alyssa's brother's name led to secrets he and Alyssa had, jokes they played, and things I would be expected to know to fool Jake. And then there were her parents, family jokes, old stories, relatives. We had lots to tell, lots to learn before we could try out this swap.

Alyssa would have to know "royal stuff, stuffy stuff and silly protocols." That's how I put it in a letter. All the everyday royal things she had to do that nobody else in the world had to waste time on. Curtsey, glance, certainlys and of courses, assuredlys and by-your-leaves. There was a hard row to hoe there, I thought.

Here's part of that letter. "...and this is the hard part. You have to pretend to be stupid for this part. OK, so there are a number of times you have to pretend the dumb thing. It's my least favorite part, really. A Duke, for example, will say that he is going hunting with my father on the weekend. Then you have to pretend to know nothing at all about hunting even though you've been hunting many, many times. So you ask the Duke a question so he can show off his hunting knowledge. Right here is when I frankly want to scream. What do I want to scream? Good thing you ask. I want to scream that I know more about hunting than this smelly old Duke, and the only reason I can't say it is because the smelly old Duke (SOD for short) is used to everyone, every day, trying to make him feel good about himself. Alyssa, it wears thin very quickly. SOD comes in many different versions, unfortunately. There's the SOD's wife who has a different set of answers she expects. And you have to feed her the same way you fed the SOD. 'Oh,' you should say. 'That's so interesting. I couldn't imagine…' And here you might throw in a 'goodness me' and an 'oh, my!' or two. The important thing is keep the flow going—the SODs in all versions know everything, and you are amazed by all their wisdom and worldly ways. So that's how it works. You are an empty cup. The SODs are all full teapots. Remember that, and you'll get along fine. I am beginning to have trouble playing the empty cup. It will be a good thing for you to try out the empty-cup thing in your head because I know, and you do too, that both of us are very smart girls full of useful things we know about how the world works. And it's easy to slip and show it. What will happen if you slip? Ah, another good question! You can get away with a few slips, but then you will be scowled at. And then the scowling will lead to 'ah hems,' and those will lead to a series of corrective pats: dear, dear, then excuse me dear, then oh deardeardear. Then you're in trouble. Dear. So practice. As I understand the principle of the thing, young girls (and boys) fit into the order of things as empty teacups. Kings and queens and dukes and duchesses and the like, these are the fullest teapots, people older than you are also fuller, then young people have to fight it out for order on down the line. Then there's the whole servant order. I'll get to that in another letter."

But Alyssa took it in stride and wrote back that it would

be worth it to be a temporary princess. For her part, new things, she said, would be the interesting part. Every day would begin with new things and end with new things. She wrote that she could imagine how thrilling it would be talking for the first time to a SOD or SOD-like personage at a castle ball, dressed in her silky gowns with light everywhere and soft murmurings of lords and ladies. She said also she could imagine that this might wear out eventually and she'd be looking for more new excitement. But the first time! The second time even! She was ready. Bring on a whole flock of SODs and she'd herd them like she did the geese on the farm. And by the way, there's one big gander that will come after you if you turn your back on him. He's mean and sneaky. Be alert. He much more dangerous than a SOD.

On my side, I could hardly wait to be rid of all that "stuff" and get on with the manure shoveling, the planting and hoeing and simple dinner and…and… Again, my mind jumped to school, how it would smell different and be like learning a new song to sing to myself every day. I thought about all this as if it would be Christmas and birthdays all wrapped into one. And if someone discovered us? And if someone made us stop. Well, I knew I had enough power to keep Alyssa out of trouble. I hoped. They would have to see that it was all my fault, and Alyssa just went along. Humm. It would be like a joke that didn't work, or a test. That's it, a test of the system. We'd be celebrated as heroes… Yeah, sure. The bad what-ifs were too unpleasant to think about. I would just think about glorious days of dirty fingernails and planting and harvesting. We'd work with catastrophe if and when it came along.

And so we learned each other's life by letters. The courier trekked back and forth with the instructions that he was keeping up a friendship that pleased me, and that the correspondence was good for royal relations with the people of the kingdom. On each end we both read and studied up on the other life until the day would come when we were both ready.

Alyssa wrote to me. "There will be some things you'll have to know about farm life. For example, things have to be done on two schedules: right now, and regularly. The right now part is when something breaks or an animal is sick or a storm is coming. Cows and horses and goats and sheep give birth at any hour, and when they do, middle of the night or not, they would like your help, thank you. They never say thank you, but you can see they like the help. Anyway, when they give birth it's messy and the sheep especially are goofy and don't seem especially present even when they give birth. This may be my own personal relationship with sheep, but they don't seem to have much going on between their ears, and birthing seems to confuse them further. Horses and cows, now, that's all very different, and when it's going right they really don't need you and you're in the way, mostly. Pigs, too, but you have to get the babies out of the way so the sow doesn't accidentally sit on one and squash it. Horses and cows, not the same problem. But when something is not right, then you are in the game up to your elbows sometimes. My father expects everyone to lend hands, elbows, knees, whatever is necessary because all animals are valuable. They are the farm's money, and everyone of the critters is 'walking gold' as my father says. You might be expected to get very gooey, so get used to it quickly. And then there's Jake. As the youngest, and a boy, he has certain privileges. But not too many. You will be expected to help keep him reasonable, to help civilize him. I already told you about his tree swinging habit. If you can't find him, look up. On top of buildings, in trees, perched somewhere like a crow looking out over his domain. He is not a tame creature. That's all I can tell you to get ready for him. What you don't expect is what you'll get. You have never been in charge of anyone else, I think. You will be in charge of Jake according to mother, but according to Jake you will not be in charge of anything but the wind blowing through trees."

And so the letters got thicker and thicker as we each tried to tell our life to the other one so she could try it out. It was hardest for me to think about being in charge of a little brother. I realized that I hadn't been in charge of anything but myself for all my life. People, other people, had been in charge of everything else. In a castle there are many places to hide a bunch of letters. But at her house, Alyssa said she hid them deep into the barn rafters where even Jake did not go.

The switch was easy. The clothes in the carriage, an arranged meeting, tea time alone in the barn, a makeup kit, a haircut, scuffed shoes. It was done. We held our breaths as we emerged from the barn and into each other's lives. No one on either side took a second look; they were so used to how we looked side by side.

The kingdom was somewhere, somehow shuddering at its foundation as its future queen picked up a milking pail and set about her chores. And the farm girl looked past the row of servants pretending that nothing gleaming and glittering meant anything to her. We both chuckled inside. But outside, we joyously began going about the other one's life. Oh, the freckles, yes. We painted mine on until the sun would bring them out naturally. For Alyssa, I brought some waxy court makeup she could use until hers faded. Done!

I can still feel the beautiful weight of the milking pail,

the grin I worked hard to stifle, the warm side of the cow where I rested my forehead. I milked the way Alyssa had instructed: always put your hand gently on the udder at first because it seems to relax the cow and tell her what you're there for, then start slow and loose, then tighten as you come down each teat like gently ringing out a wet cloth. And Alyssa walked off a princess, magic transformation made by clothes and how she held her head and the charged air of authority she radiated around her. Right from the first instant, she seemed to have it down perfectly.

Alyssa's first words as princess were these. "See to it that the family has sufficient money to repay them for the refreshments and the trouble of our visit." I almost broke out laughing. She stifled a grin. "Oh and a little extra"—and here she royally gestured a circle with her hand to show how much more—"for their time. A farmer's time is money, and we should recognize that." And then more gestures, maybe one or two too many, but she certainly had the right idea. Draw all the attention to herself to keep it away from the farm girl she left behind.

My new life began like this. "I'll get that, mother," I said to my new and puzzled mother who was cleaning up after the royal event in her yard. "Let me," and she handed me the chair she had brought out from the living room, the chair that was never sat on by any royal behind or any other behind during the whole event. I began cleaning up like any good daughter and looked around to see if I could find Jake and begin my stewardship of his life. My mistake was looking around on the ground until I remembered Alyssa's Jake-spotting instructions: look up. I began with the barn roof, then the shed, and then a rustling in a big beech tree drew my attention. There he was like an exotic bird, flashes of his red shirt between the leaves.

"Jake," I called up to him. "Give me some help, please." The leaves stopped shaking. He was in hiding. "I have something for you if you help me." I had brought one shiny, unpolished gemstone from the castle, something that could be found anywhere but just rare enough to interest Jake. I patted my pocket. "It's right here." And I went about my work. I could almost hear him thinking and wondering high in the tree. One thing about wild critters: they are curious.

Then slowly, branch by branch he swung his way to the ground, wiped off his hands on his pants, and edged over to me. Here was the test. If he was to be fooled, it would have to be now.

He eyed me cautiously, like a deer, skittish, as if something was wrong, but he didn't know what. I got the feeling that my disguise that seemed to fool Alyssa's parents and the entire group of adults, had not been enough to convince Jake. It seemed he was sensing something besides my appearance, maybe smell or something else, and all was not quite right in his brain. I pulled out the stone with my back to him and held it up to the sun so that yellow and blue flashed in his direction. I waited. And I could hear him slowly coming up behind me to get a better look at what I had for him. I turned the stone this way and that to get the most flash; it was as if I had some tasty morsel and a hungry creature was snuffing the air behind me. And then there he was by my side.

"What is that? Is it for me? Let me see." The moment of truth.

Jake's attention was completely on the stone. I reached out and put my hand on his mop of hair and its twigs and leaves he wore like a wild crown. He relaxed and reached for the stone.

I explained matter-of-factly, "I found this digging in the

new part of the garden. If I find more I'll save them for you too."

He held the stone up to the light, turned his back and walked off with his treasure, swung casually up to a lower branch in the maple and perched there as if all were right with the world. He turned the stone to catch the light, and I knew I had passed the first test. Next time I might need more than a flashy stone.

Chapter Three

What was going to be a trial week, we agreed, quickly turned into a trial month. Thirty very exciting days of trying out all we had learned of the other's life. It was like playing a role in a play but every day, all day long. The life in the castle turned out to be so regulated that it was very easy to fit in. Alyssa wrote me that it was "like just picking up your feet and being swept along in the routine."

I found the farm life exactly what I'd always wanted but more complicated because of the decisions I had to make every day. Sick animals, my "parents'" expectations indicated to me by silent nods or raised eyebrows, care for my brother that was expected and not explained, all these and other things made my part more difficult, I think. And once, well, once Jake blew the whistle. He broke out all his doubts about me at once.

"You're not my sister," he blurted, pointing at me. "I don't have to do what you say. You're not my sister, anyway." I had asked him to do something, something he didn't want to. His opening shot stopped me in my tracks.

I held my breath. The truth of Jake's words hung in the air as if an elephant had wondered into the room and sat by the fire. Jake was eight going on nine and seemed to see right through the whole charade from the beginning. But it was as if with the gift-stone he saw it as a game to play. Until that day. "You can't tell me to go to bed. You're not my sister."

My new mother saved the day. "He's overtired," she said. "He had a big day and didn't slow down once. I'll put him to bed tonight."

I exhaled. The air came slowly back into the room. Everything normal again.

And after that one time, Jake seemed to accept me completely, as if he got the idea of the game and now went along with the rules peacefully. But I knew right there behind those brown eyes lurked the key to the whole charade. He could pull back the curtain any time he wanted to, and the play-acting would come to a crashing halt. I gave him half of my dessert, his favorite, sweet egg pudding.

I woke each morning eager to get my hands into the dirt, to feel the weight and sway of the shovel as I cleaned the barn. The hayloft was guarded by an owl, and each morning I greeted the owl with small hoots I hoped might be taken for hello in owl-talk. Then the three cows, one by one, I addressed as formally as it is possible to address a cow. "Angie, you're the best." I stroked her between the eyes. "But Cindy, you are the second best, and I have noticed that once in a while, you're actually the best. For a time. And then you're second best again," I babbled diplomatically because the cows, though new to my acquaintance, had quickly become my favorites. "And June. Oh, June, June. You try, but then, well…there are circumstances, I know. The other two, talk and… I know. It's difficult being the third one sometimes." I rubbed June extra hard between the eyes and scratched a twitching ear, and she seemed to realize that being third had somehow made her special, more special than the other two.

I went through my morning ritual with giggles; I admit to finding myself hilarious. All part of my new joy, I figured. When I was a princess, I had never thought of myself as quite this funny. Owl, manure, cow, and then one more thing. Always one more thing I looked for to improve the barn: hang the tools straight, oil one harness, pull a weed near the door, clean the small windows built into the foundation so the light came through clearly. And sing. The animals all seemed to like hearing my singing as if it reassured them that everything was fine in the barn world. Alyssa had said that she sang while working, and she left me a list of songs she knew. I knew four of the ten songs on the list. I would have to learn the other six if we could keep this going. So I sang Alyssa's songs, in case anyone else was listening. But I also sang made-up songs about owls or cows or chickens. One of them went like this.

When hoot owls have a fancy party,
Do they call the mice?
When owls run out of party food,
Do those birds think twice?

Are the guests the next to be on plates
With parsley and small crackers?
Would a mouse's tail fill the bill of fare
For those hooty, owly snackers?

Not such a wonderful song, I know, but I just made it up right there in the barn while not one but two owls looked down on me from the rafters. The next verse had cats in it and something about them eating mice too, but I can't remember all the words to that part. The barn to me was a better sort of castle where all kinds of things came together: work, animals, and fine rich smells. Every day the smells and sounds changed from the day before: the hay dried out more, the cows belched and pooped their contribution, the sparrows and swallows and finches flavored it all with songs. I loved to walk into the barn door slowly like a guest sneaking in. I suppose that's where the song came from. I'd be as silent as I could to see if I could catch all the creatures being themselves.

I wanted this life to go on forever. No dressing for formal occasions, no shoes that pinched, no smiling at people I found awful and odious. I felt as if I had been leading the wrong life and now had magically returned to the life I was born for. My fingernails quickly chipped and became impossibly dirty. I tried a princess habit of cleaning, but it took too much time. I tucked my hair into a cap to keep it out of my face. This life felt as right as wind through trees, water over stones. I thought the month would be up too soon.

And so I began to wonder how Alyssa and I could make the swap into two months…or longer? I didn't dare think it: how could we make it permanent? Alyssa would have to love her new life as much as I loved mine. She'd have to love the pinching shoes and fake smiles and old men with their nose hair combed out into their moustaches. How could she? There was the banging around of guards to show they were vigilant, the flapping castle flag outside her window at night, the cold breakfast table in that ghastly, empty room instead of the warm farm kitchen. How could she, indeed?

I wish I could bring dragons and monsters into this story. It would be so much easier to explain the world falling to pieces. We could have one medium-sized dragon eating an important person—wouldn't matter who—and then everyone running around excitedly and the kingdom coming undone. The monsters and dragons that appear are only the kind that are pictures of what we imagine we're afraid of. You know, what's under the bed, in the closet, lurking in that shadow behind the old tree. These are the hardest dragons to slay because you can't see them. And it turns out that sometimes the things we can't see or, worse yet, the ones that are right there under our noses every day are the most dragonish!

Dragon number one was a gentleman. At least that was his title in the world of the castle. Arbuckle Pemberton III was a cousin, twice removed (or maybe a second cousin once removed), of my mother. His only real problem was that he didn't have enough to do. His whole life would have been saved if he had found a passion; even a silly pastime like collecting history would have saved him. But he had gone round the bend without even seeing that the road was curving. I grew up with Arbuckle lurking there in court, climbing up on chairs, being insolent, trying, oh trying so hard, to be a *Someone* in his distinguished and historic family of *Someones*.

He had a rat face that contained an awful hole of a mouth. He was lipless as a lizard, and the lizard/rat combination startled people who were meeting him for the first time. But the zoo of his impression continued. He had long thin feet covered by rare, brightly colored leather sewn into shoes for him by the court cobbler. The effect was something startling too, as if half of his being had been turned under to prop up the rest of the menagerie that was his face. Ears? Oh, yes, like two bats unfolding from roosts. Hair that he'd purposely pompadoured into a tower and then powdered a gray-blue not seen in nature. And so the total effect was that natural and unnatural had joined into the perfectly absurd. When he wore his yellow shoes especially, he gave the impression that a paint pot had exploded nearby. I, and many others I assure you, snickered behind our hands as he paraded into sight with all the concocted confidence he could pretend to muster. A one-man parade on a holiday no one knew about. Not much of a dragon viewed this way, but dragons, it turns out, have many disguises.

His role at court, he figured, was to set style. His ears,

mouth, feet, hair and ears were actually quite normal if he had let them be. But each one was part of his plan to start a style in court. If you had been a fly on the wall of his bedroom in the early morning, you might have seen a perfectly pleasant young man sleeping in his bed. But when he woke, he powdered his hair, propped out his ears, painted his mouth into a hole, made his face rodent-like and tugged on a pair of his silly shoes. Ah, I'm sure he thought, looking at himself in his full-length mirror, there it is!—everyone will want to look like this soon.

At court we watched him move quickly from chair to chair so as to appear to be everywhere at once, the faster to make his style seem unavoidable. And each day at court he would try to make a convert or two: shoes, ears, hair, makeup. But progress was slow, and if he, for example, had instead taken up hunting or horse racing or the plight of the unfortunate or education standards and practices, well, none of this style-pretending would have happened. Setting style was such time consuming and heroic work for him because of having to sell it daily to the largely disinterested court.

But then he found a hobby—Alyssa. Something was not quite right about the princess, he noticed one day. Alyssa wrote down the discovery in her letter about the same time Jake had declared me a fake. It was somehow her eyebrows, or something. Somehow about her whole head, its shape maybe, its topography had changed. Anyway, Alyssa reported to me that he studied her and studied her from across the room. He even forgot to circulate from plush chair to plush chair in the court. What...was...it...about... her...? She was a young girl. They change. Every day. But... Alyssa said it was unnerving at first. She thought certainly he'd found her out. But his dressing weirdness combined with his new gawking weirdness combined with his overall unseemliness, well, the combination was tolerated at court since his family had been so prominent, so full of important people at one time. But his behavior was wearing out for everyone. And with it his standing at court.

Then Arbuckle began to let his style campaign go by the wayside. He had less and less interest in the hard work of the pompadour, the bat ears, the rat face, because Alyssa began to take up all his concentration. What was going on with her, he obsessed? Alyssa reported that all his world seemed to come tumbling down: the courtiers paid him no attention without his style campaign, his rather regular features blended him into the court, and he failed to move chair to chair and so became more of a piece of furniture himself than a person of substance.

And here is where I have to fill in what I think happened because Arbuckle was not a stupid person, just one who didn't have enough to do and so had gone rotten, like fruit left out in the sun. Arbuckle thought and thought and thought, and at night he lay in bed staring at the ceiling and thought more, two more thoughts. I think it must have gone that way. He was always thinking and thinking, though, as we already know, the results were sometimes not very valuable. And then it must have come to him that the princess had somehow been replaced with a look-alike, well, an almost perfect look alike. But why? I'm sure he began with theories: who would benefit from the scheme? Enemies, that's who. Enemies of the realm, of wealth, of privilege. The substitute was sent into court like a worm into an apple. He would be vigilant; he would wait and pounce. And this is what I think was going through his mind, because Arbuckle Pemberton III was a child of great and devastating privilege. I like to think that his birth kept him from tending plants or other useful work, and so that led him astray. My birth almost did. I got lucky, and luck on top of privilege is a very useful combination.

The other monster was Jake, not so monstrous at first. A shiny stone, a pat on the head and he was (sort of) tame. How could he be a monster; he was just a kid brother? But Jake was a boy who wanted. He wanted more than a farm, than the simple meals, than dirty knees and Sunday dinner. But he was very young to know much more than that everything he found around him seemed sadly lacking. Tired and worn out. I could see quickly that each day he took a deep breath and went through the motions. But always like a silent song or a voice in the wind, he wanted, wanted some vague thing or things that weren't there. That's all he really knew: what was absent, that's what he wanted.

Each day the voice, the sad song, seemed to get a little clearer. And this clarity in combination with his immediate realization that I was not his sister any more, created a small whirlwind that grew and grew, gathering sticks and dust and then small stones as it whirled. He wanted. I think the wanting was why he always climbed into the highest places as if maybe he could see what he wanted from up there.

Meanwhile I was finding everything I wanted in crops and goats and chickens and horses and sheep and cows. And kittens. And puppies, of course, in season. Live things everywhere that seemed to rise up out of land itself.

I marveled at the obvious things: you fed the cow alfalfa and there was milk. You kept cats to clear the barn of mice, and there were soon more cats. The goats took care of themselves, nearly. And sheep wanted you to think for them, so there were the dogs to do it. The rhythm of living things making more living things as fast as they could—I felt I had lived my whole life waiting for this rhythm to kick in, like it was always just over there where I suspected it could be, but I was not quite part of it. There had always been the gardening, but that was just a taste. Now I found myself filled up every day with chores that seemed more like play and a tiredness at night so perfect that I only had a moment to smile to myself as my head lay on the pillow. And then it was morning. And I could smell the earth from my window, hear the animals, taste the wind. I always had suspected this happiness was here, and my bones were glad every day. So, of course, I understood Jake's vague and unfocussed wanting. I had it too, but I had found what I wanted by coming down, down from the castle to the fine, brown dirt.

Jake was somehow empty. I was full. Summer was almost over. There were the crops to harvest, the preparations for winter, and then there would be school, another world I longed for. I saw the other children in the school visit. And all summer I saw them again on market day in the village. Alyssa had given me the friend list: close friends who knew secrets, friends who were just smile-and-wave friends, and then the others. I would have to make my way with these by the time school came after the harvest.

Market days, the first one especially, were tests. I had Alyssa's descriptions of friends I should greet and how warmly I should greet. I thought of it as a game, but as the first market day approached, I returned to the letters that Alyssa wrote to help me. There was Angela, who was not an angel, according to Alyssa—whatever *that* meant. There was Elizabeth who was never Betty or Bettes, but always Elizabeth pronounced A-liz-a-beth, not E-liz-a-beth. Angela was interested in boys. Elizabeth was not. Then there were the three sisters, each a year apart from the others. They moved together like a flock of birds. If one was angry, all were angry. Keep one as a friend, and they were all your friend. Noted!

Market day was bright and warm, the stones of the village scrubbed and still wet. An old man scurried from place to place cleaning up after the horses and cows brought to market. The sheep and pigs were sold outside the village in a special pasture. Children were running everywhere getting more numerous by the hour as sellers set up stalls and stopped to gab with friends. I kept close to my father, worked with my head down at first so I could peek out and see if I recognized anyone from Alyssa's descriptions. There was the trio of sisters across the way, but they were hard at work unloading vegetables.

Then suddenly behind me, "Alyssa! Alyssa." And there was Elizabeth. I would try out what I had learned.

"I haven't seen you since the wedding in the spring," I began. "Wasn't that fun? The dancing. I thought it would never stop."

Elizabeth, without a hitch, began to tell me about what happened after we left the wedding and her family stayed. "...and then the two soldiers got into some kind of argument and they had swords and everything. And someone tore her dress on a nail. Oh, and then the constable came too. I couldn't tell what happened then because my father and mother scooted us all out of there. Said it was time to go. And we went, but I could hear something noisy happening even as we went down the road home."

Let's see, I thought. After the wedding there was something...oh yes, the brother with the broken leg. Or was that the other girl, Angela? I couldn't come up with the answer right away, so I thought it was best not to bring up the broken leg at all. Elizabeth was a talker, so I let her go on. And then *she* brought up her brother's broken leg and how she had all that extra work to do. I shuffled through Alyssa's letters in my head, mentally flipping through the pages for the next clue. But I didn't need to do that, it turned out. I could just listen and talk back, and soon Elizabeth had to help her family set up. And I had learned that I could pick up Alyssa's life by mostly listening.

Jake cruised the market, I assumed looking for a high spot. And very quickly he found one, up a fountain wall where the village water ran from four spouts so four jugs at a time could be filled. Above the spouts was a carved lion and perched on its head was Jake like a gargoyle. Mother and father apparently had every confidence that Jake was safe perched up there, or *anywhere* he perched. He had convinced them he could seek out high places and study the world from above.

Then the three sisters came over. I wasn't sure which was the one I knew best. The tallest one, I thought. She looked like the leader. But it was the middle sister who seemed to run the trio. I had learned from Elizabeth not to offer too much and then just go along with the present conversation. The market by this time had begun to sing with voices of all sorts, "Onions, carrots, herbs and thistles. Beautiful ham, a fruit pie for your table."

The sisters, too, immediately accepted me as Alyssa, and I actually felt like I had now become her, got inside the story of Alyssa and become part of it.

The middle sister, blonde braids poking out both sides of her head, sealed my confidence. "OK, Alyssa. We all have birthdays coming up. We'll see you then." And the first market day buzzed past with heaps of mushrooms like tiny umbrellas, garlics in braided bunches, and tiny new red potatoes with dirt still clinging to them.

Chapter Four

Alyssa wrote that the life at court and the duties of being a princess were endlessly fascinating as long as they didn't repeat. I remembered them as achingly repetitious, so she must have been experiencing them a different way. She was a very smart girl, and maybe the newness of everything, every ritual, every historical necessity was like dessert to her soul. She worked very hard to learn from my letters why the blue sash was necessary for the evening meetings of councils because blue was the color of the first sash used 800 years ago by ancestors so old they didn't even have portraits on chamber walls. Red was for daytime frivolous parties because...there was the history to learn. Black was only for... Yellow could be substituted for red when... It all seemed to tie together.

The more she learned, the more the parts fit as if the whole meaning of the castle and its history had been spun out like a spider's web. There were old men and women to consult if something didn't make sense. And after they explained, the pieces fit. This because of that, they said. This cape, this hat, those shoes, the tiara—all spoke in silent ways to the task of keeping all the people accepting the story that we told about ourselves. And woe be unto any break in the story, because the fractures would grow and grow (this had happened to a neighboring kingdom, they warned, and *they* all ended up living in the woods and eating worms, it was said). And that would be the end. Protect the story and you protected civilization itself, they said. Glory to ritual and glory to story.

I knew what she was going through. I had been trapped by it all my life and every day, so that the whole spider's web that ensnared the castle seemed to make sense and, yet, be frankly silly at the same time when you're in it. For Alyssa, though, all the flash and glamour, responsibility and self-importance seemed to please her. I wrote to her that even the empty gestures were useful threads binding together the nation. Better her than me. I liked the sense that seeds gave me when they grew into plants.

The whole summer for now-princess Alyssa bloomed with newness and the fall too. But then a repetition began to set in, as I thought it would. Do that same curtsey again to the same old gentleman, the same young dance partner, the sashes of many color codes. And then she could see that the newness would come to an end in time, and she would have to do the same hundred things over and over. She wrote to me that it might be time to trade back. Or to stay permanently and move into the princess part that would grow larger each day instead of repeating.

That letter I was both expecting and fearing. I had come too far by then to give up what seemed glorious to me each day, my new life. I had doubled the size of the garden by digging the warm dirt and turning it under. I kneeled my way through the weeding and wore my knee mud badges proudly. The smell of new dirt seeing the sun for the first time! The surprise of the worms as they turned around and headed back into the dark soil. I laughed to myself that I could see the surprise on my worms' faces—no faces, of course, but the ones I imagined.

But Alyssa found that getting in touch with me was getting to be much harder than she expected. Here's why. A princess, as I well knew, had to do three things that might lead up to a fourth that would then present the possibility of a fifth that *might* then present the opportunity to do what she really wanted—like contact me. I knew that particular tangle and the ways out of it. But that part of my life, that cleverness that had taken all my years to develop, that set of skills and miss-directions, she didn't have yet. It should work like this. She must suggest an afternoon meeting that would then lead to a series of similar meetings that could then, possibly, become a school visit or another farm visit and then... Unless, of course, I was, by chance, tiring of my new life and was trying to get in touch with her. Maybe that would be the easiest way. If I could visit the castle, then we could consult. But my peace was Alyssa's anxiety, my daily joy her impending sense of doom.

Part of Alyssa's discomfort, the main part: Arbuckle Pemberton III was doing more and more noticing. Alyssa's walk seemed to plod sometimes, he noticed. When she was tired, maybe, or just not paying attention. Sometimes, just for a second, she'd seem to lose focus at state events, stare into space as if her mind were elsewhere. And since Arbuckle had dropped many of his "style" affectations, he now blended in more with crowds and could get closer and closer to the princess. Something is not right, must have echoed in his mind: I will find it out and reveal it at the right time, the right place. As I said, he was not stupid. And not being stupid presented Alyssa with another set of problems just as the shine of court life was wearing off for her.

Jake continued to want, and he didn't know exactly what. I would pat him on the head (Alyssa had never done that before; she always tried to hug him), I read him stories endlessly until he fell asleep, where before, Alyssa had a strict two-story bedtime rule. And sometimes he could hear me outside humming a song Alyssa had never hummed before as I went about chores. He liked the owl song. The sheep dog, Rex, had once growled at me before I made friends with him by feeding him table scraps. Jake was another level of difficulty. If only I could have fed him table scraps to get his loyalty. Sweet egg pudding was good enough in the short run. But that was not to be enough, eventually. Sparkling stones and pudding only work for a short time, it seems.

Arbuckle and Jake are my dragons in this story. Dragons are unpredictable and mysterious. They guard treasure and breathe fire, and no other animals do. They have scales like some creatures but don't live in water like scaly critters do. So we keep dragons around for story purposes. But both Arbuckle and Jake made good dragons.

Of the two, Jake was the biggest dragon because he was the most dragon-like: he was unpredictable, and he had some idea of what treasure there was to guard. As the youngest member of the farm family (cats and dogs and goats not counted), Jake enjoyed the privilege of being the darling of everyone—Alyssa, his parents, even visitors. Jake was cute and small and growing every day so that each day he appeared newly made, and the sunshine seemed to follow him across the meadow and up any available tree.

On the other hand, Arbuckle was a smaller dragon because he could barely maintain any dragon-like qualities. His attempts at style, while they kept the court laughing behind his back, were at least some claim to prominence at court. "There he comes," they used to say. "Let's see what goofy costume he has today. Oh, the black lips! Now that's an improvement!" And so forth and so on.

Arbuckle was sensing that Alyssa was not actually the princess, and this was just a gift to him from the gods of fortune. No one else seemed to have noticed a thing. Arbuckle began walking around each day smiling on the inside over the deliciousness of what he knew, or at least suspected. He would take his time to reveal the truth as soon as he had proof. He would call everyone together,

King and Queen included, and make the monumental announcement. He would hire trumpets and banners. The princess would be revealed, and he would be the hero. I have known him all my life, and this is how he thinks. But first he would have to know and discover and be sure. Find out where I had gone. That was the key. Time would be bided, Arbuckle Pemberton was thinking. He would be thorough and ruthless and…right!

With two dragons in one story, there's always the chance that they'll meet and destroy each other. Or another chance is that each dragon will cause its own kind of mayhem and unruliness, and kerfuffle.

Alyssa wrote me that she worked each day to be more and more princess-like, as if she sensed somehow Arbuckle's plot.

She said her day would go like this.

"May I be of service, Arbuckle?" He lurked, she reported. Always he lurked.

"Oh, princess, yes. I was just wondering if you remembered that story of your mother's oldest cousin who fought at the battle of…? What was it again? The battle of…?" He opened his eyes wide inviting her to supply the battle. "Oh, you know it perfectly well. You were always so good with the history. The battle of…?"

And she had learned to counter his attempts to trap her.

She said, "OK now, Arbuckle. Put your mind to it. Try to think of facts around the battle you want. It's a valuable technique for remembering. Think of the place first. Then the stories from that battle. Then…that's it. Keep trying. You'll get it. Go ahead. Think hard."

And eventually he had to give in and name the battle, and she would claim a victory for having helped him remember. Then, she wrote, she would study up with the history tutor and next time Arbuckle lurked, she'd pounce.

"Arbuckle, ah, there you are. I was writing to your aunt, our aunt, I suppose, though the blood's gotten thin at that end. Anyway, I wrote that we were discussing the battle of Shornsteby, and the loss of our own dear Adrolone, 'the unkind,' wasn't he? Androlone the Unkind? How he saved his reputation by one final act of selfless valor." She said she was laughing on the inside as Arbuckle's eyes grew bigger and bigger at her command of family history. Hummm, he seemed to be saying to himself. I didn't think she would know these things. But, Alyssa wrote, he was never fully convinced, only confused. She'd settle for confused.

Another time, she reported, Arbuckle had taken his lurking further. She could see his shadow outside the room she was in working with her tutor. They had moved on from history to a kind of complicated arithmetic. The shadow came closer, maybe to hear better. The shadow crouched down. All this she could see in the mirror. The shadow smelled of suspicion and how far Arbuckle's idle mind had gone astray.

The tutor was cheering her on. "So if we count by fives—five, ten, fifteen—then the number one is actually five, isn't it?" She was trying to keep track of both the shadow and the lesson.

"What? Five is one?"

"Well it is *like* one if we're counting…"

"But it's not one. It's five. Unless ten is going to be two."

"That's it! Good work. Then ten *is* two. And fifteen is…?

"Three!"

At this point, Arbuckle sneezed. And sneezed again. The lurking was finished; the shadow disappeared. After the lesson, Alyssa discovered a broken pencil tip outside the door. Arbuckle had been taking notes, gathering evidence, she thought, to try to trip her up.

On the whole, I much preferred my own dragon, Jake.

No lurking, just little fires he started accidentally.

By courier we agreed that we would each stay exactly where we were, where we were happiest, and not try to switch back and forth just yet. That is, unless there occurred some emergency where we had to act quickly. Or unless either one of us changed her mind. Alyssa, though she had doubts, had become very fond of the rich food of the castle, even the ceremony and empty pomp at court; she wore her duty like a cape, she claimed. But also it was tiring on her, she wrote. That cape could get heavy. She didn't know if she could do it for life, but also she could feel herself changing and moving toward the princess business more and more each day.

I had become very fond of the day and night fullness of farm routine. Each of us felt herself slipping deeper and deeper into new identities. How long could we keep going? Would we just each become the other? I was sure I could blink my eyes and spin in a circle to complete the transformation and act as if I had been on a farm all my life. I was afraid Alyssa would need more magic spinning and blinking and maybe some magic dust to make her change complete. And, of course, would we get away with it? There lurk the dragons, of course.

Chapter Five

It seemed almost impossible for Jake, farm boy, and Arbuckle Pemberton, court fop, to join forces for any reason whatsoever. But they did—dragon sniffing out dragon. Arbuckle noticed that our courier—and the couriers were always the soul of secrecy—left the court occasionally and journeyed off in the opposite direction of all the other couriers. And Arbuckle had the advantage—he always did have this, even as a small boy—of being nosey. The lurking instinct! No other way to put it: he was constitutionally nosey. Why, he asked himself, would one courier, though not very often, leave the castle to the south, down river, when all the court business was located to the north where all the other couriers carried their messages?

And so in crafty disguise, he planned to follow the errant courier and see what he could see. I knew well that news at court was always welcome, and gossip or rumor was always trumped by real news of the outer world. Nothing gave status at court like bearing a piece of news that reeked of reality and newness. And no piece of news struck the eardrums and hoisted the eyebrows quite like a revelation that began, "...Oh, and by the way, I just found out that..."

Arbuckle had only once before tasted the joy of the revealer's privilege. He had announced a treaty of some importance, days before it was made official—he had, of course, lingered outside a closed door to steal the information—and ever since the shiver of joy that ran through him had made him long for another such shiver, another taste of glory, while all eyes and ears bore down on him, HIM, for details. I believe that all the high-style nonsense he worked at each day was really just a replacement for the attention he craved. The attention his ancestors had received for their faithful service to the state, that was what he really wanted. Blue hair, black lips, until recently, had worked as a substitute. Now discovery was everything.

I learned later that this is how the two dragons met.

Arbuckle followed the courier. He borrowed a small donkey, dressed in country jerkin and shoes, and rode in secret. The first time out, the courier, riding one of the castle's finest horses, quickly out distanced him and disappeared over a hill. But Arbuckle could almost taste the court's attention, and so he got aboard the donkey and spurred the poor beast so hard that it collapsed at the top of a high hill. He rolled the exhausted creature into the ditch and trotted himself down the road until he saw the courier in the distance glancing this way and that until he was sure he wasn't being followed. Then the courier set off across a field toward a farmhouse just visible in a grove of trees.

Arbuckle hid himself and waited. And waited. And finally the courier came back across the field, rejoined the road and made his way back toward the castle. Arbuckle, followed the trail the courier had left across the meadow and burrowed into a forsythia hedge near the house and waited to see who or what could possibly have been the goal of the courier's message. While he waited, the yellow flowers slowly rained down on his head and shoulders every time he moved.

All this secretive business I know because Jake could see most of this action, and he couldn't wait to tell me later. Jake is the key dragon here.

And that was how Jake found Arbuckle, sitting cross-legged in the bushes hidden from everyone except a small boy. Arbuckle's head was by this time a garland of yellow petals and his lap a potpourri of flowers and twigs. A small white butterfly had alit on one of his knees: a coxcomb of nature was Arbuckle. An omen of things to come. I imagine it went something like this.

"What are you doing under our bushes?" Jake asked in the deepest voice he could muster. "What do you think you're going to steal?"

Arbuckle spun around to see who was talking but saw no one. Jake had climbed a tree and was speaking from behind a large patch of leaves, hanging by one arm and one leg from a crotch in the branches like a small gorilla.

"You're under arrest," Jake said in his deepest voice. "Well, I'll call the Bailiff. I'll call the sheriff. I'll call my father." I think I might have been next on his list of authorities, but he probably didn't get all the way to me. "I'll have you in chains, you know. We have chains right there in the barn. We could easily clap you in chains." Jake sometimes liked to find out what there was to say by saying things.

Arbuckle continued to look around from under the bushes, and not seeing the source of the voice, the idle threat (for Arbuckle was well connected in the legal world of the kingdom and feared no consequences for his actions, no matter how illegal), he crawled out from under the forsythia raining yellow flowers, and stood up. There was Jake like a ripe fruit hanging in the tree. He climbed higher, out of reach, and then shook his finger at Arbuckle as he had seen his father do many times, and announced, "You, you don't belong under our bushes."

"And you," Arbuckle pronounced, "you don't belong hanging in a tree like a small monkey. Come down at once. I have questions for you." Arbuckle clapped his hands together to get the dirt off and then finally wiped them on his grubby pants and straightened his clothing and primped his coiffure out of habit. "Now! Now! Come down. I wish to speak to you immediately."

And so the meeting did not start out well. But slowly Jake descended, circled the tree cautiously, figuring he could always run away faster than this old rag man, and then stood with his hands on his hips and said, "Well, ask then. But be quick. I don't have all day to be gabbing. *I* have work to do. I don't know about you." Jake eyed the raggedy man with contempt.

Arbuckle, used to the trickiness of the king's court, the ins and outs of diplomatic misdirection and folderol, began by asking Jake his social status, his relationship to the farmer, and then the state of the crops, whether those apples were ripe yet, how many cows there were on the farm, and a number of other irrelevant things so that he could eventually get to the heart of his questioning.

But Jake, after cautiously beginning his answer as a child might to any adult, decided he'd had enough. "Stop," he said, holding up one hand as if he were directing traffic. "Just stop for a minute. My turn." And he proceeded to ask Arbuckle who he was, and who did he think he was, and why did he think he could ask all those questions and why he was on their farm in the first place. I had seen Jake operating in full protector-of-the-farm mode before. He was quite formidable for being eight years old.

Arbuckle finally admitted he was Arbuckle Pemberton the Third from the court of the King, the King's wife's cousin (though he was really just some version of a second cousin) and a powerful man in disguise on a special information-gathering mission. So there. Both fell silent slowly circling each other, barely moving their feet in a dance of grass kicking and shuffling without any music but birdsong and wind through the leaves. A crow orchestra joined in. Then a blue jay, never to be outdone, chimed in his hacksaw caw.

"OK," Arbuckle said finally. "Alright. Here's the question. Why has a king's messenger come to your farm regularly? Who does he talk to? Why? What is the..."

"Whoa. Hold your horses," offered Jake. "I never see a messenger, King's or anybody's. What messenger? When? Talking to who?"

And again they fell silent, having each asked the same questions. It appeared as if there was an extra dose of questions and not enough answers. And all the time each one had his suspicions about, first, the princess, and that something was amiss, and, second, his own sister, and that something was amiss. The two, boy and (sort of) man, jousted without words. Then each fiddled with his pockets as males, I have noticed, are taught to do at a very young age: thumbs hooked in pockets, back pockets checked and straightened, hand finally stabilized in one pocket. I have seen this male-dance many times and always marveled at it.

This strange pocket dance might have gone on all afternoon, but around the corner I came, and both stopped and looked at me. Of course, I recognized Arbuckle immediately and put on my best play-acting set of skills to become thoroughly the Alyssa I needed to be. I tugged out a hank of hair from my cap to appear more disheveled.

"Jake, your chores await you in the stable." Darn, I thought. That was too much princess, not enough sister and contradicted my hair ploy, so I added, "And get a move on. Don't let the barn door spank your behind." I shooed him with a small shove. That should do it, I thought. Jake seemed relieved to be released from the uncomfortable encounter and scurried off toward the barn. "And you, sir. May I be of any help? Some food, then be on your way.

We have no work here for you. I'll find you some small thing to eat, but then be off." Again, I thought I might have overdone the princess superiority and underdone the forceful country girl. So I added, "No time to dither or shillyshally. My chores are calling me too. Do you need food?"

Arbuckle began to circle me, study me. I thought I better strike first.

"Sir, you must move along. If you have no business here, shoo! I don't want to call my father. He's very unpleasant about strangers on his farm. He always leaves them injured." Of course, my new father was the kindest, most gentle, man in the whole world. He really would find food and probably some better clothes to give a stranger, but I wanted Arbuckle gone before he had any more time to study me. Still, he circled slowly as if he might be moving away, but he kept cocking his head to the side like a giant crane waiting for a fish. He was calculating something, something not good, I thought. His habit of scheming seemed to drip from him: narrowed eyes, rubbed chin, ears slightly wiggling.

After a moment he said, "Oh I think I can be on my way. But just one thing, if you don't mind. Would you say the wind is freshly blowing? Or blowing freshly?"

No, no, no, I thought. We had spent too much time near each other in the castle. He'll surely see who I am. I reached one dirty hand up and wiped it on my cheek as if I was scratching an itch. A little camouflage, I hoped. I tugged at more hair across my forehead. I was hiding myself right in front of him. But finally he stopped the gawking as if there was something he was supposed to know here but couldn't quite see. Something that his grammar trap had sprung in his beady little mind. I decided best defense might be a little offense. "Shoo," I said again like chasing off a dog that had been bothering the chickens. "Shoo and be gone, sir. I have no more patience for the scruffy likes of person like you. On your way. Now! Be gone..." And I would have gone on and on, I suppose. I have done it before. But he seemed to give up.

And Arbuckle again said he didn't need food. That he'd be on his way. That it was kind of me to offer. And he pulled his hood over his wig and looked sideways from the depths of the hood to re-gawk at me. I could see his squeaky little mind at work. My hair was wrong, my skin sunburnt, my hands calloused and grubby, but something...something... But he only said his leaving words, brushed the last flowers from his rags and pretended to make his way off the farm. Actually though, I could see that he stopped in the first depression, a drainage ditch, and hid. He hid until he thought I was gone, until he could see that Jake was again moving about the farm, and then Arbuckle slithered his way along a bank of trees and pssted, and then pssted again to get Jake's attention. I had gone up into the hayloft and spied on them through a crack in the barn wall.

Arbuckle was charged with intent. "OK, boy. Jake. One question. Is everything about your sister the way you think it should be?" And Jake, after rubbing his chin the way he'd seen father do when pondering something important, allowed that maybe there was something different about her lately, but he couldn't put his finger on it. Couldn't quite figure out if she was different or just being a girl, you know, like girls do; first one thing, then another, like girls, you know. Mysterious, changeable, powerful strange. Sisters. Older sisters.

Jake loved games and games with secrets even better. From where I watched it was hard to tell exactly what was going on in his mind, whether he was just fooling around with Arbuckle to kill time, or whether he was taking the bait Arbuckle offered—the sister puzzle.

Jake said, "She's right. She's good to me. She really loves that garden of hers. So, yes, she's right, the right one for my family."

Arbuckle sighed loud enough for me to hear from the barn, a sigh from deep somewhere in his bones. He was a man caught in his own fits of curious distrust of the world; he was growing tired of being that way. Standing in the sun on a strange farm with an impish boy and a threatening girl—surely this was not the life he was made for. Like his ancestors, he was made for much more important things. I had heard the whole "alas-speech" before. But still—something was not right with the way everything lined up crookedly. Things were not in their proper place. Not at all! A courier to a farm? The girl who was somehow not what she seemed? This boy who seemed to live in trees?

And the peculiar cooperation was born. I guessed at this boy-pact, because I could see them nodding together, Arbuckle gesturing to the wind as was his habit, Jake closer to the vest, hand in pocket.

They, together and seemingly all at once I imagined, must have exhausted the topic of the sister and the princess and how strangeness had suddenly descended on both of them at about the same time. And, hmmm, what could that mean? They would stay alert. They would tell each other if something important turned up, something unusual and revealing. Jake would watch for the courier. Arbuckle would try to follow one again. Something was rotten, they certainly agreed. Something didn't smell quite right. I watched them shake hands. More nods.

A few days after the appearance of Arbuckle, I breathed a sigh of relief. Though Jake seemed extra nice, almost as if he were pretending to be something he wasn't, more grownup or something, things went back to normal. Neither

Eugenie nor I needed the courier; we returned to settling in to each other's life like cupcakes into muffin tins. I began to ask for my new mother and father's farming books: pig breeding, woodlot tending, the many uses of manure, the proper way to trim a fruit tree. They didn't have many books. Much of what they knew about farming, it turned out, had been passed on from the fathers and mothers who came before them, and the best way to tap into this information, I found, was to get them talking about what they were doing as they did it. I had to be careful not to sound too pushy when asking, just casual interest. I found they would talk easy about mending harness, preserving the harvest, tending sheep through their birthing, horses' hooves, chickens' beaks, and seed saving if I worked my questions into regular conversation. When it rained I talked drainage. When it was hot, soil moisture. When it was windy, the thickness of wheat stalks and bend resistance.

We'd sit by a small fire in the evenings. The days were getting warmer but the night chill still had a pinch of winter in it. My father's stomach would rumble after dinner and he would sometimes snooze in the rocking chair sitting straight up and seeming to look into space with closed eyes. Jake was busy on the floor taking something apart, something that looked like a wooden puzzle with small iron pins. My mother made a pattern with fine yellow thread on a disk of linen. I could only keep my eyes open by wanting so much to remember every second of this, this tiredness and fullness. My hands were a little sore from weeding, my back warm with muscles well used. I smiled at my cracked fingernails and how they had been sacrificed so that plants could grow. I wanted to fill myself up with the smell of smoke and the flash of yellow thread and the snorts of Jake as he wrestled his puzzle together. One light hanging from the ceiling kept us all under close watch.

For days at a time I forgot the palace, the deceit, the pretending, and even, sometimes late in the evening when the beautiful tiredness of work crept into my bones from the long day, I forgot who I was. And wasn't. There was no was or wasn't, only becoming. For flickers of time it seemed I was always Alyssa, and that far off over the hill, that other girl always had the bother of court dealings clanging in her ears. And I had the soft wind in mine.

In the palace, I could imagine Alyssa sighing as her head sunk into the fine down pillow and the sheets whistled their silkiness at her. She was now growing more delighted to spend the day in gestures and appearances and protocol. She was finding home too in another place, another skin that fit better each day.

Chapter 6

And one day, after a time, it happened, of course. It had to. There were so many changes that one thing had to crash into another, the wheels had to begin to wobble before they fell off, and like all complicated things, the pieces began to fly off in all directions. It could have started in any number of way. So many things to go wrong. The courier was an obvious place, but it wasn't him. We used the courier less and less. And it wasn't that one of us forgot her Ps and Qs, her shoulds and ought tos. No. It was a small thing, an accident really, something that normally meant nothing at all. A small thing that was huge. Arbuckle spied from his place in court and came up with nothing. Jake burrowed into the family and waited for me to reveal myself, but I didn't. You'd think that two dragons, two girls and a fragile world would be the deadly combination. But it wasn't.

It was water. Water that rained on places fair and foul. Water that collected in the ditches and made its way into the great reservoirs of the earth. Water that made it possible to have both farm and palace. Water that had been clean and delicious one day, and the next became sickening.

On the farm, what was left over—food scraps, paper, broken tools, manure—all found a second home: scraps to the pigs, paper to burn for heat, tool parts used again, manure to the fields for fertilizer. But in the palace, there was an old man in charge of making sure all the waste that wasn't wanted—human waste, animal waste, kitchen waste, old clothes—all were taken far away from the King and Queen's sight and smell. We all called him "Carrier" because that was his life. Carry it all somewhere else. Do something with it, something not near here; that was the court order. Waste was supposed to disappear. And while the Carrier was young, he hauled it far from the castle and buried it deep. But, as he got older, the burial got shallower and nearer until at the end, the Carrier didn't have the energy to go far. Finally, he pulled his loaded cart just out of sight of the castle, into the closest depression, the one I remember from a summer picnic when I was very small, a sort of sheltered place of blue and yellow wildflowers and deep cracks in gray rocks. And so the great waste of the castle crept closer and closer and lay next to the great river that fed the rest of the land. Then one day the sickness came to farm and castle at the same time. Some bomb ticking inside the waste, some careless and unhappy soup there got cooked into a disaster.

Sickness was everywhere, and everywhere was the monster of more sickness coming. An old aunt once said that only when the monsters are defeated can we begin to argue about other things. She always used to say that—one finger in the air to show how important this was.

Arbuckle and Jake were suddenly joined by more than their mutual curiosity about the girls who seemed slightly strange in their lives. The farm boy and the fop were joined by something like the haze that surrounds a moon sometimes, the strange aura that could make any normal thing eerie. That was us, Alyssa and Eugenie—neither one quite fit in the box into which we had been stuffed by birth, and so we each sent out a haze of strangeness. And the two suspicious males didn't know what to think of this, but they *did* know that they couldn't stop feeling that something was truly wrong. Then came the bad water.

All throughout the castle was the sound of sickness: groans and retching, scurrying to deal with diarrhea, and the word "alas" and sighing as the business of the kingdom ground to a halt. King, Queen, knave and kitchen maid alike groaned. The religious leaders of all sorts blamed hidden sins, vengeful and spiteful gods, ill-aligned planets, great wheels of fortune that had spun to the dreary bottom. But for all the explanations, no one thought it was the water. Water festering in a shallow grave just outside where the castle dipped its barrels of drinking water; water that sang a sad and doomed song that was carried down the river to farms and villages. Even dogs and cats were not lively any more. The birds left suddenly as if they had seen something from the sky that made them abandon the kingdom. The cows and horses slowed to a stop and waited, their eyes glassy. Chickens slept in trees waiting for a chance to fly off to somewhere else where there was no sad song. The farms groaned too.

Jake and his family—all of us—took to our beds: no appetite, no energy, sick stomachs and, finally, the disorder of not caring whether we lived or died. All of us just wanted to sit and stare instead of work and laugh. The sickness seemed everywhere—the old folks called it a miasma, bad air wafting from some dark place. Our thirst drove us to drink even more water, and the water sang its evil song in our blood. The whole kingdom was sick. When the farmers didn't bring food to markets, no one ate. When the wind blew a tree down across the road, no one came to clear it. I felt as if something had come in the night and taken my bones.

Finally, just when it appeared the kingdom was ripe for invasion by its war-like neighbors, something happened, an accident really, that brought the truth to light. Alyssa in the castle and me on the farm, each in our own way discovered the bad water.

I crept out slowly one morning to see if I could tend my garden. It seemed the plants called to me. My knees buckled, and I sat in the farmyard crying. I could see my garden from there, but I had no energy as if the light inside me was slowly going out. I started to crawl because I could see the garden's wilt, its thirst for water and need for care. I felt as if I were crawling to save a crying child. I pulled myself along until I came to the edge of my garden. Most of the plants were wilted but one, a kind of bean that never needed much water to grow, was almost glowing with health. It had shed the few dried leaves that happened when it was being watered and now reached for the sun and flowered everywhere to create more beans. I sat and stared at this dry-lover, this sprightly green thing among the brown ghosts. And I wondered why this one? Why was the healthy one the one I *hadn't* watered?

I remember trying to think, like trying to think and fall asleep at the same time. The bean plant would flicker brightly and then be gone through my tears. I wanted to sleep, but the idea of that one plant singing out to me kept me awake. Why that one? How could I be that bright green bean climbing up the poles? I felt, instead, like the crispy brown leaves on the dead plants.

I dragged myself closer to see what magic was there. Around the base of the hardy bean was a dry circle I hadn't watered. Every day when it was warm, I had to carry heavy pails of water from the well, and I learned very soon to use water only where it was absolutely necessary. The bean did nicely without much water. Something in that water had changed, I thought through my fog. The water was part of the three golden parts of my garden: sun, fertilizer, water. And now my golden triangle had come undone.

About the same time in the castle, Alyssa had dragged herself up to the window of her bedroom because in her sickness she said she longed to feel the outside wind and sun on her face as if somehow the cure would be there. And she saw from her tower that one short valley away from the castle was a dead zone of swollen dirt where the Carrier had unloaded his carts into a shallow grave. No insect or animal stirred there. No plant waved in the wind. There, next to where the river sorted itself out into the land and ran off to the lower kingdom, there was no light but dry emptiness.

So, it was the water, we decided as if our brains were the same brain. We thought, the very first thing, that the other one should know about it before we told anyone else. But there were no couriers who could still walk or ride with messages. So we, with one mind and one face, thought—I have to get well and tell the other. I made a strict plan to eat fruit to get my water and drink, like my bean plant, none.

I tried to discuss the water with my very ill father and mother. Thy lay together in bed facing the wall. My father groaned. My mother waved her arm weakly in the air. "Take care of Jake, if you can. Try whatever you want," she said, and rolled over.

"The water," I started to say. But she was groaning too, and not much fire was left in her.

And so I hauled myself into the orchard where I gathered apples with great difficulty and pressed out the juice to drink. At first, all I could manage was to suck the juice from fallen apples. My thirst was yelling at me to drink and drink, but the image of the bean climbing its poles made me stay with only apples. Very soon I was feeling better and set out to tell neighbors. No one listened better than my parents had. Listening to young girls was not going to be the way this plague was solved, apparently. They were so used to the council of the King and the wise men that it was very hard to hear a young girl's advice. I would have to think of some other way to show them.

In the castle, there was a similar reaction. All the

counselors told Alyssa that she was just a girl and the King had many people working on the sickness problem—men of great wisdom, of religion, of astrology, of magic even. And so she planned her own withdrawal from the sick water. As thirsty as she was, she looked for other ways to drink. She found grapes and ate them greedily for their juice. In two days she was walking among the groans and cries of the castle, helping others. She began to scour the castle, then the countryside for anything to eat, anything except the water.

Alyssa plotted her escape to tell me the news on the farm. But finally, no plot was needed since there were so many sick people, so little attention to anything but stomachs and bowels, and Alyssa found she could walk right out of the castle and make her way toward the farm without anyone caring a jot.

And so each of us on her own, wandered toward the other and met on the muddy trail that dipped along the river and then folded itself up into the hills between farm and castle. Alyssa wore her hunting clothes, and I wore my second-best dress in case I had to go all the way to court and talk my way in. For the moment, we looked as if we had switched back. When we spied each other, we hurried forward and waved and helloed, though quietly, each mindful that we should not be seen together even in our new disguises, but also certain that no one was abroad these days of sickness.

We both began to speak at once as if we were one person talking to herself instead of the two fierce and separate girls.

"Alyssa, you go first. After all, you are the princess now. I'll listen first because I am the loyal subject of the princess," I said, thinking how unimportant all that business seemed now among all this raging sickness. Both of us paused, eyes open in delight and began to laugh at what I had just said.

"OK, OK," Alyssa said finally when we were able to stop laughing. "It's simple."

And then both at the same time, as if we were being directed in some great choir, "The water makes people sick!" We had the gift, but no one would accept it. We both knew the one thing that could stop the suffering, but we could find no listeners to tell it to.

Again, it was some time before we could continue because we had so surprised ourselves by speaking as one. It was as if we had absorbed enough of the other's life by living in her place that we had half become her. And now two half-lives were meeting in the middle. We just had, of course, really met in the middle. Spoken at once in the middle. Shined our two faces into the mirror of the other.

I was tanned, and my hands showed the daily work with nicks and scratches and broken fingernails. Alyssa's nails were painted and elegant, not having lifted a finger in a while, and her pale skin seemed fragile out here in the countryside. And now I had the freckles.

She said, "We are the two that have to become one voice." It sounded so important, so much like a proclamation that we both laughed with surprise and delight.

"Say another one," I joked.

"Alright. How about this? Two stars must shine as one beam from the skies!"

"Not as good, actually. Try again."

Alyssa thought, conjured up her new princess powers and announced, "The kingdom needs the power of two girls to bring one truth. Let's away!" And then fell to giggling. Even in this sad, sick time we were feeling the lightness of our new lives. The kingdom was groaning away all around us, and we sat making up silly lines out of a play we were inventing. It was the silly lines, though, that freed us to help. The talking, the liveliness of two girls scheming in a field to save our world—well that was glorious stuff. I realized I hadn't said more than a few words to anyone for too many days. And without words, even though I felt better, the world was pouring out slowly in front of my eyes like thick molasses. Our silliness hatched a plan, and then another plan and another as if we had warmed the molasses.

Alyssa proposed a grand scheme. "We can lead the way." And here, she did that raised-finger thing my great aunt did when she made wise statements. "We know what's wrong but don't have any listeners. How do we change that?" And then she launched into a very complicated plan. A lot of it was going right by me, but I could see she had picked up the castle way with big words and grand schemes.

I stopped her. "Without a place to speak from, some high place, I don't know who will listen to us. How do we change that?"

"That's what I was saying. That was the plan."

I could see we were talking about the same thing two different ways. I had no plan, just the sad fact that no one would listen to us. Alyssa, with the same fact, had a complicated plan that included all the people who wouldn't listen to us now. If they heard us, then her plan might work. But no one was listening.

So we stared over again and sat and talked about what we could do regarding the water problem, how we could help each other with fixing what was wrong, how we might get an audience that wasn't too sick to listen. The castle's wealth, the farm's connection to the land—each had its power. We talked and planned until the sun was just touching the hill and about to leave us in the chill of evening.

"Oh, I have another one," Alyssa said, holding up one wise finger. "Two..." But she got to laughing, then stopped. "Two girls getting better each day." I raised up an apple I had brought from the big tree where Jake made his second home. "Two girls to save the world one apple at a time." And we toasted ourselves, the apple tree, and the world we would save. We left with no great plan except to think of ways to find listeners.

Chapter 7

Just out of sight, lying on his side with father's spyglass, was Jake, nearly recovered on the apple juice diet I supplied him. He moved the glass back and forth between the two of us. It was clear which one was his sister. He saw her every day. He had only seen the princess once, that day in the school and barnyard when the royal visit had occurred. But now he could see what he hadn't seen then. The two girls looked something alike if you adjusted for…what? Clothes? Suntan? Hair dos? His scowl seemed to ask, why would his sister meet with the princess again? Each one was dressed like the other one. And they were jabbering away as if they were long lost friends. What is this about? Jake was entering deeper into the mystery. He'd ask me straight out. No. I'd tell him some tale. I always could do that; he liked the tales. He'd accuse me of… Of what? Of seeing the princess on the sly? So what? He'd ask his mother…no, his father…no. Ask them what?

And so Jake watched the sun dip too, and what he saw was that we hugged, that I wore a dress and the princess hunting clothes, and that we went back to our places having discussed at length something Jake could not hear. Jake hurried back home ahead of me certainly going over and over in his head what he could do to solve the growing mystery. And what did it have to do with the water sickness? Surely the two things were not separate. I know that he believed he should try to talk to Arbuckle, and they could figure something out together.

Arbuckle Pemberton III was not feeling well. In his chambers he had given up style and fashion, court intrigue, and even the peculiarities of the princess in the name of simply reclaiming his bowels from the galloping diarrhea he'd had for days. Nothing tasted good enough to eat. Only a vile thirst crept upon him every day so that he tried in vain to take in enough water to replace the water he was losing each day. Arbuckle was not the only one in his condition in the castle. He'd been, he felt, reduced to a tube into which you poured water so that it could come out the other end.

Alone in the castle now, Alyssa told me she was the only one moving among them trying to help others, bringing rags and comfort and always trying to talk people out of drinking the water they all craved. She brought them grapes and juices of all sorts, but few wanted to try. Not one listener. At least I had grateful Jake.

Nothing tasted good. Only the monster of thirst roared at them all. Some of the very old were gone already. The very young, babies, were nursing and seemed best off. The children were wretched but strongest. The castle smelled to high heaven of sickness and fear. Arbuckle sighed. Against one wall were cabinets of his clothes hanging in rows and legions, but they held no fascination for him now. Court was not meeting. Intrigue was dead. Something was making the whole world wrong, out of joint, discombobulated. He bemoaned that something awful was creeping under the entire fabric of the kingdom's existence. Our enemies will soon come down upon us, he thought, and end everything we have built. The world was sick in more ways than one.

Everything his relatives built was sliding away. For Arbuckle felt he hadn't really had a chance to be considered one of the builders of the empire. His father and his father's father, yes. His uncles and aunts all had stories of conquest and building, how each had brought some piece to the construction of the great civilization itself: the civility, the order, the art of protocol and negotiation. The

Great Society was made by others. For him. And now he must make his mark, too. I had watched him as we grew up becoming more and more desperate, desperate to make his contribution somehow, even if it was only silly style. The water had him down and not caring.

Jake, on the other hand, felt nothing so complicated. His sister, the real one, the one from before, the one who occasionally took his side, had changed. Or been changed. Or had been kidnapped and replaced with this other version. To him, the sickness was unpleasant but was only part of the more important things wrong with the world: the farm didn't work, the animals were listless, his parents were very sick. As he got better, he began to climb again. From up high, things seemed almost normal.

Alyssa and I had decided we had to risk being discovered if we were to save the kingdom from itself. "The water! the water!" we would say. And some person, some agency would have to listen and do something about the water. Clean it, stop the poisoning. Something. And so we went back to our places, farm girl and princess, to spread the word. But "some person," and "some agency" proved, as we suspected, very hard to find. The people surrounding us were more than just sick; they were immoveable stick-in-the-muds. They were so stuck in the world they had known before the sickness that they only wanted it back the way it had been, so they could keep on doing what they had been doing before. And doing it *the same way.*

In the castle, they yearned for the smoothness of daily duties and positions in which someone was superior to someone else and also inferior to someone—everyone but the King and Queen. They knew their place and cherished it. But the water had changed everything, and none of them knew it was the water that made everyone equal.

Those who could walk around consulted the holy men, then the holy women, then, finally, the unholy witches and diviners and readers of chicken entrails. Anyone, they said, help us! Anyone, Alyssa and I both found out, except two young girls.

And as you might expect the information from the holy and the unholy was often at odds. The church said it was sin, and so God's punishment had come to them for their sins. Which sins, the people asked, willing to change, to give up whatever it was that offended God? But the holy men and women could not agree which sins, and so they decided that giving more money to the church would be the best place to start. Let us, they said, save the kingdom. We'll talk to God and get back to you. The less holy, on the other hand, offered up fate itself (a complicated thing, it turned out) and said the kingdom would just have to tough it out. And, by the way, it wouldn't hurt if large sums of money could be made available for advanced predictions and expeditions to consult other less holy experts in other lands.

And so money seemed one of the few points in common. Out came the treasure. There were golden plates, jewels in all the important colors of red and green and blue and some in yellow. There were even jewels of no color at all, jewels that only reflected other light and sparkled. There were valuable horses and cows and sheep that one could spend like money by trading. There were rare and silky cloths that slid across the hand like water. And so the kingdom spent and spent and remained sick.

On the farm, word trickled down from the castle that one had to spend money to make God relent and forgive everyone. But lacking gold and jewels (though in possession of a few animals, but those were needed every day) and other means of making God happy again, the farmers began to make fires, in the old way, fires that heaped up all things they thought might be offending God and requiring Him to punish his people. Old bones (this made the dogs unhappy) were heaped up, and broken furniture and cracked shingles. All broken or useless things were added to the heap and burned. The particular bonfire on our farm roared up to the sky with its message of making the old and bad into smoke that would make it new and good. The logic seemed clear while the real cause lay in the sickening water, its load of unpleasantness that made people sick and unable to work the land. But the farmers, like at the castle, repeated the best old ideas they could think of and made even larger fires. More of the same would be better! The night glowed with atonement and hope for a better tomorrow as farm after farm tried to burn its way into grace and salvation and health.

Still the land lay sickened, and both of us, each avoiding water in her own way, tried to tell everyone that the water was making them sick. The people, both farmer and king's court alike, repeated harshly to us that the water had always been good to drink and it still was. Something else, something hidden from puny human ability to see, was making everyone sick. They said, and don't worry your young heads over the matter, the adults would ferret out the error and correct it. Even now much money was at work to aid the act of discovery, and it wouldn't be long before the problem would be solved. Both Alyssa and I heard the same message in two different ways. But it was clearly the same: you girls are not the answer. You can't be because you never were before.

And so the risk, the risk of having to go back to our old lives, the risk of being punished and publically humiliated, was going to have to be greater each time we met.

We began to try new things: elaborate disguises,

complicated schemes including miss-directions and fake reasons. Alyssa's complicated first ideas, those funny plots, came around again. This wasn't going to be simple.

"Mother," I said, "I have to go to other farms and help. I'll be gone a while. But I'll be safe on the roads. Everyone is sick including the robbers and highwaymen." And mother who was too sick to argue, waved her hand and marveled again at my good spirits and energy and said yes to some vague plan in a vague place with my vague details. She was beginning to believe that my recovery had something to do with my apple diet. But when I tried to persuade her that she would get well too, the old thinking got in the way. She gave me her blessing with another weary wave. She couldn't find the place in her mind—though her heart knew—where her daughter knew better than every adult both high and low.

"Mother," I said again, and put an apple on her bed, "I'll be back very soon. I love you and father and Jake. Jake is getting better. He'll bring you whatever you need." She looked at me with her tired eyes and smiled. I could see she knew that something would have to change soon. She was so thin and worn out from the sickness. She seemed to know that some kind of end was going to have to lead to a new beginning. And she sighed deeply and put her hand on my shoulder. I moved the apple closer. "It'll make you feel better. Jake can always get you more, if you want more."

Alyssa reported the castle maladies. "Oh, the smell," she reported to me. "With so many people in one place at one time, the smell gets worse every day. No one had the energy to clean up. The waste of all sorts builds and builds just outside the castle walls."

"Do they believe you about the water? I just know it's the water. We're living proof," I added. "Of course, if we came to them together and stood there healthy and strong and told them we got all our water from fruits, they'd have to take us seriously." She lowered her eyes and sighed.

"They would know," said Alyssa. "As soon as we stood there together, they'd make us go back. They'd see what we had done. Do you think they would punish me? You might get a scolding, but I would be…what? I'd be taken to court, my parents ruined. I'd be thrown into a dungeon and…"

"Worse," I said in my most serious tone. "They would be certain that we had caused the problem, that we had messed with the proper order, and that messing was what brought down the sickness on the land. I know they would. They can't see farther than their own blind superstition."

"The ends of their noses."

"Their own belly buttons."

"The insides of their own eyeballs."

And we took off again and began laughing the way we did in the field. I think we did this to keep from imagining the real difficulties that could arise from our switching places. I didn't really know what "they" would do. Alyssa was right, I would be fine after a lecture or two. But she might not be fine. And her family? I didn't know, and that was the truth we avoided by goofing around with noses and belly buttons and eyeballs. What would it take to change the way so many people thought about so much? And what could two girls do? Everything, it turned out. *Two girls could do everything.*

And so we agreed we'd try to *show* (instead of tell) people that somehow the water was making them sick. And off we went. We couldn't even change places temporarily, we decided, since now I looked the part of a farm girl with my tanned skin, rough hands, and even my long stride that got me about my chores efficiently. And Alyssa would have a hard time standing among the farmers with her soft hands and un-sunned skin. We had become each other in many ways, and going back would require undoing all the changes we had worked on over a long time now.

Meanwhile, Arbuckle was still sick and lifeless, lolling around from chair to chair, moaning and sighing, Alyssa reported. But each minute of weakness something in him grew more resolved to solve the problem of the land and establish himself in the pantheon of founding fathers that was his family. He resolved to find that farm boy again and get him to work to a common end. Then, finally, he would dismiss the boy and take all the credit for his discovery. I knew his thinking. He held tight to the belief if he could find that something was out of order in the kingdom, something in the wrong place, some error had occurred, the cause of everything wrong would be clear. And the cure. Set it right and everything would return to normal and he would be the hero. His whole life had been arranged by this principle of "correct order." I was a part of this "order" business myself until I replaced it with how a plant loves light, water and food.

"Psst. Psst. Psst!" Jake heard outside his window late at night. "Boy! Psst. Come out."

Arbuckle, dressed in his best disguise but barely able to stay on his feet with the sickness, cracked the quiet night air with his plea. "Come out, boy. I need you." I could hear them both from my room, and I thought, this cannot turn out well, these two, ill and whispering in the night.

Jake felt the pull of his bed because though no longer sick, he was young, and he was very fond of sleeping under the best of conditions. But after a while and the psst-ing and loud whispers outside his window growing even more insistent, he roused himself, put on clothes and reluctantly slipped out into the night.

"Now what?" he said, after they had moved away from the house and into the shadow of the barn. I could hear them perfectly, their exaggerated whispers. After their first meeting, Jake had no fear of Arbuckle having completely dismissed him as a human being. If they could be useful to each other, so be it. The guy was a goof. A bag of straw.

Arbuckle coughed. "There's something wrong with the two girls, and you and I know it. Don't we? Don't we? What is it? What exactly have you seen with your sister who looks something like our princess?"

Jake thought for a moment. "Well, Alyssa is nicer than she used to be. And..."

"No, no, no. Not nicer! Is she...does she...?" Arbuckle looked around for the words he needed. "Is there anything you *know* that might explain...?" I could hear his frustrated whisper getting louder and more anxious. "Maybe what she says, or something she mutters to herself or maybe a spell or incantation or magic animals around her?" I almost laughed out loud. Arbuckle had been consulting the soothsayers and spell mongers that, according to Alyssa, now had free run of the castle. She said that when nothing else seemed to work, these folk multiplied in the walls of the castle like mice. He continued, "You know, there might be some little thing she does that she didn't do before. Think! Think, boy. What might be out of line, you see? What is there to know now that you didn't know before?" His voice now had broken the whisper and was climbing higher and higher like an angry bird. I could see that he had put his hand on Jake's shoulder and was pressing him more and more.

Jake didn't know. What he did know was not something he could put into words; it was a sensation he got around me, a feeling that too much had changed. The sister was one way, then she was another, almost as if the smell of her or the color of her eyes was slightly off. He had tried talking to his father about this one time. One time. I overheard them in the hallway. Father had said that girls go through changes that boys...well, boys do in different ways, but girls...well...they change in bigger ways. Other ways than boys. Ways that are...well... And then father had asked him to do some chores, ones he usually did himself as if he were trying to get out of the question.

Jake told Arbuckle this. "I don't know what it is about my sister. I don't know what's wrong. But it's something, and every day I get the feeling that today I'll find out what it is. But I never do, do I? And so I wait for the next day and start over again. Waiting. I guess that's what I'm doing. Waiting for something more to happen, and then I'll know. But I don't know what I'll know. What there is to know. That's the problem. I don't really know *anything*. Well, I know she's not sick like the rest of us. But that's it. Oh, and I'm getting better too." All this came tumbling out of him like a flock of birds exploding out of a bush.

Arbuckle said that the princess, among all the court people, seemed not to be sick either. Then he proposed a plan. They would work together to see why the girls weren't sick. That would be the first part. The second part would be to see what was wrong, why they didn't seem exactly right anymore. "Those two know something. That's why they're not sick. Maybe they are causing everyone else to be sick! That has to be it. Maybe they are witches. Why else would they be the ones walking around well, while the rest of us throw up our guts and..." Arbuckle had let go of Jake and was now walking in ever larger circles in the moonlight by the barn. Into the shadow, back out into the moonlight. In and out like a crazy horse carving on a carousel that came and went. His circles got bigger until Jake seemed to have had enough and bolted up the big apple tree and disappeared into the leaves. Soon I could hear the munching of apples from up near the top. And Arbuckle, still muttering, staggered off into the pasture moonlight.

Jake might have decided to sleep up there. I don't know. I went to bed wondering what it would be like to be a witch, have magic spells and strange, curled up things in bottles of yellow liquid that I would use for potions. All I had, though, was knowing that the water was making the kingdom sick.

Chapter Eight

And so the clouds gathered on two sides of us: (1) Arbuckle and Jake spied and peeked and tried to find our secrets (although they already knew, just didn't know they knew), and (2) like Cassandras who knew something no one would listen to, Alyssa and I had shouted our message about bad water into deaf ears.

It had to be something more mysterious, Arbuckle was sure, and he favored the supernatural. Like everyone else, he thought that water was water. Anyone could smell that it was fine and hold it up to the light to see that it was clean. Something had to be out of place for the world to have turned so wrong. And so, as with his theory of fashion, he clung to what he thought he already knew.

And we two kept trying to tell everyone around us every day that the water was the problem. We tried to think of more ways to show it than just the two of us being healthy. Cleaning up the water would be the solution. But the priests prayed, the diviners continued to cut open chickens to read the message of the entrails, and the heaven gazers charted the stars and planets and the moon in their nightly peregrinations. All reported to the King that something was amiss, and they were hot on the trail of possible corrections. But everyone kept drinking the water and their great thirst increased with every loss of fluids out of every bodily opening.

The kingdom languished. The King and Queen most of all because they accounted themselves, in a most royal way, chiefly responsible for discovering what was wrong and correcting it. The head of the army suggested they attack a neighboring state that must be doing something evil on the sly to cause the sickness. Reports from spies said that the neighbors were not sick at all. War would be the answer the generals said.

The priests maintained that an unhappy God could be pleaded to through sacrifices and the raising of prayers and exotic smelling smoke up to the heavens. God would fix everything when the kingdom had sacrificed and offered enough. Piles of incense were gathered and prepared to make a holy stink to the heavens. The altars were prepared for sacrifices.

The soothsayers and astronomers joined together to look to the skies in a different way than the priest, and they each drew out elaborate diagrams of heavenly connections, birth conjunctions and orbits that would give the kingdom a picture of its woes; solution to our woes would be triangles and rectangles and overlapping spheres of influence.

And so it was inevitable that, besides Alyssa and me, the farmers, who looked mostly to the land except on Sundays, that the farmers would be the first to pay some attention to our pleas to clean up the water. And some did, beginning with father who began to hear my pleading about the bad water. My health and my refusal to drink water eventually came up and smacked him between the eyes. Ah ha, he thought at long last. Maybe the girl has something there. Nothing else works. And he began with himself and avoided the water. He, in a week, felt much better with a diet of freshly crushed apples and watermelon. Then he took the water away from mother, too, who seemed quicker to believe him than her daughter. But better late than never. And in time my new family stood in glowing health among the plagued population of the kingdom.

But it's always difficult to get a king to listen to a farmer; it always has been and maybe always will be. Our one family beamed the light of health from the countryside, but when father tried to get an audience with the king, he was turned away by the kingdom's most fervent (but sickly) advisors whose very jobs depended on the King's belief that they alone held the key to making the sickness cease. And when father went to his neighbors with his health news, they groaned and asked him who did he think he was to answer the big question that the finest minds in the kingdom could not answer. Just *who the hell* did he think he was? So no matter how he paraded his healthy family before them, they moaned and returned to their illness because this farmer, their own kind, was acting without authority or standing or agency among them. It seemed everyone all along the line had trouble convincing the next level of power.

And then Jake, now healthy and slurping watermelon every waking minute of his day, made his discovery. His sister did not just seem different. As he suspected all along, I was not his sister.

The two and two he put together was a combination of accident and good observation. As his health improved, he began to watch me more and more closely as I went about my chores or sat at the dinner table. At Arbuckle's urging he studied how I walked, how I ate, smiled, sneezed—everything! I could feel his gaze, almost as if Arbuckle had made Jake his deputy whose job it was to note everything and report back to the sheriff. Jake was on the lookout every day that passed. There were Arbuckle's eyes flashing somewhere behind Jake's.

When did she start doing that, Jake wondered? Did she always do that? And on the same subject he remembered that before the sickness, I sat up stick-straight at the table while the rest of them leaned into their food. I ate while daring the large gap between plate and mouth, daring the gap where food could fall in my lap. I poised the food there above the plate then executed the move smoothly without a slop or spill. How did I do that? I could see him across our table, now as we all tried to regain our health. He watched me like a frog watches a dragonfly.

That was the clever part. The luck part was a little more complicated, but without it, Jake might have been left mulling my exotic table manners and never seeing through the disguise.

I was fond of the kitchen garden where I raised the fresh vegetable and herbs used every day for meals. Oh, I did other chores—the stable cleaning, the care and feeding of chickens, keeping the hay troughs full for the animals. But the garden was my special delight. Anyone could tell. I sang when I worked there before the bad water came. I hummed my way across the yard on my way there. I couldn't help it. I would begin to smile as I gathered my gardening gloves, trowel, shears, kneeling pad, string and pegs for planting straight rows. I felt like the plants I cared for, as if we both were drawing power directly from the sky. My step was light with the anticipation of my favorite work. It was hardly even work for me because I doted on it, and my fondness for dirt and plants alike glowed like rays of sunshine into the shadowy places of the world. My work—I couldn't hide it—was my kind of worship.

Not that Jake knew any more than that I floated off to the garden every chance I got. And there I hummed and sang to the plants, the dirt, the butterflies snuffling among the flowerings. Jake saw me fill up there on some unseen and lavish love that he couldn't quite understand. It all looked like work to him. He was glad for my garden joy, I think, since he didn't particularly like the drudgery and the bending and kneeling. He would rather be fishing the pond and catching turtles, sidling among the saplings to see if new bird nests had appeared, swinging from branches.

One day as Jake was skulking past the garden to make his great escape to the woods before father found something useful for him to do, I was there half sticking out from the tall green potato plants and let out a sharp cry and then some words Jake had never heard before. I had punctured one finger with a sharp splinter and yelped my everlasting pain. But it was what I said that brought Jake up short. We are not entirely in control of the words that come out of our mouths in such agony.

"By my sacred ancestors and all their holy God's blood…" I swore. "Damnation and fiddlesticks… Oh my…" And then followed a string of words Jake had never heard in his life. And, he was pretty sure, his father and mother had never heard in their lives either. He had heard his father swear in the barn, had been party to what his father called the male initiation rite of learning to curse, a skill, father maintained, that the finer nature of women would not need but that males in their baser states could cultivate. And what I had flavored the morning air with, that was not ever in the cursing lessons.

He heard parts and pieces and shards of things: *locus ubi puer conciptur* (of which he understood nothing but the sound), and then blackstick, and sarding, and he thought he heard "Christ's fingernails" and something about God's bones. And a mishmash more as I filled the air and stood up holding my hand up with blood darkening my raised glove.

Jake stood, mouth open, hearing the wailings from the depths of my aching finger. And then I turned and saw him and flushed red from my ears inward that rose crimson up my cheeks and left my nose aglow. I stuttered and looked at him and muttered parts of things and looked at my shoes. Then I pulled off my glove in obvious pain and hurried away toward the house with the blood flowing down my hand. I had, for the bloody moment, completely gone back to being a princess favoring the garden air with my song of pain, my *very educated* song of pain.

Jake couldn't have known what he had just seen and heard, as if he'd suddenly been transported to some other kingdom where he floated like a stranger among the foreign language. I could hear him repeating what he remembered. He knew he wasn't getting it right, but he repeated over and over the parts he could. He would take this to Arbuckle to find out what I had said. This is what Arbuckle had been asking for. Spells, imprecations, insults to the order of decent folk.

Arbuckle, for his part, had decided that a high thing sent to a low place, a low thing raised, a thing from the left sent to the right, a hidden thing suddenly revealed, a thing that should be hidden somehow abroad in the air—he thought of the combinations of wrongness that he could set right. And he plotted. Find the boy again, he thought, and begin there.

So Jake and Arbuckle met again, around the back of our barn where I could hear them from the loft. And this time Jake had a rush of information he blurted out as soon as Arbuckle came into sight. Jake had worked hard and long to remember what he could of the string of noises that spewed from my mouth when I punctured my finger. He repeated them all together in a rush of half-remembered sounds. Arbuckle listened like a dog hearing a far off, very high whistle: he cocked his head to the side, his ears visibly raised, his eyebrows furled.

Then he said, "Again. Say it all again, boy." And this

time Arbuckle narrowed his eyes and pursed his lips until his face seemed to collapse on itself in concentration. Jake recited his litany.

After several repetitions, one slowed down, one slowed *way* down, Arbuckle broke into a grin, an expression so foreign to his face that it seemed transplanted from some other face. He announced: "That's Latin! That's Latin, boy, and you have it down pretty well. Congratulations. That's your first Latin!"

"But my sister doesn't know Latin. I don't think she does. She wouldn't. We don't have Latin in school." Jake scratched his head, puzzled. "No Latin. Where would she get Latin?"

Arbuckle announced, "Who knows Latin? The church. And witches. I think they do. They would, you know. They know things that most people do not." Arbuckle was hearing a choir of his own suspicions ringing in the air. "I was right. They are both the same kind of witch!"

Jake was very impressed by Arbuckle for the first time. Magic and witches and spells and unnatural things, these were interesting. He was feeling very proud of having remembered my words well enough for Arbuckle to decipher them. The code was broken. What was hidden was revealed. "Just think, my sister, a witch! Wait until I tell her I know. She will be so mad that, that…her ears will fall off. They'll put up a sign outside our house, 'Beware of the Witch.' They will put up *two* signs!" he pronounced finally and with great firmness. The prospect, it seemed, was very pleasing to him as if he might take me to school on a leash to show me off. Maybe he could parade me around the village on market day. "Maybe I could *sell* her." But then he scowled. He had gone too far. I was very nice to him, nicer than Alyssa was in her sternness. He thought about it. "No, I won't sell her. But it will be very interesting to show her off."

Arbuckle was shaking his head. "No, you won't sell her. You won't *anything* her, boy. She will be taken to the castle where they have people who specialize in this sort of thing. Ministers, I think. Or sub-ministers at least. These people have experience with dangerous sorts like these two girls. I'm not sure if either one of them is the real princess."

And I could hear him now speculating on the rewards he would get, surely a post at court, and, of course, treasure. And, his painting done for the wall to join his famous ancestors.

Arbuckle was already cashing his new information. The world was out of joint because farm girls begin to speak Latin. *Contra naturum,* against nature itself. First girls! Then *farm* girls! Speaking Latin like some sacerdotal malediction, like some evil priest hurling down souls and raising up wickedness. Was it a sign or the cause? Arbuckle returned to his Latin learning, the language of all things holy. And Latin used out of its natural order, of all things unholy! One talked to the everlasting in the language that the everlasting understood, good or wicked.

But as he began to ponder the philosophical ins and outs of the pieces of the world wrenched from their proper places and Latin flowing from the mouth of a farm girl, Jake broke his bubble of thought.

"I don't think she's my sister," he announced in a voice matter-of-fact while he picked a piece of grass to chew.

Arbuckle jolted out of his fuzzy pondering. "Well, of course not. She's been occupied or some devilish thing. She's been transported or transmigrated...or transmogrified or something. It's her, but it's not her." And he went back to his cogitating.

"No," Jake insisted. "It's really not her." She isn't Alyssa. My father was wrong; it's not girl stuff. You're wrong, it's not that she's occupied or any of the trans things. It's just not her." Jake sighed deeply as if all there was to say he'd just said. His plans of sister-on-a-leash fleeing.

"Can you prove it? What makes you think this...this... thing you think?"

"She's too nice to me. She takes my side in everything. She never pulls my ear. She never gives me a Dutch rub or Vandal burn on the arm or a flick on the nose. That's it. She's too nice to me and has been for a long time now. Alyssa was my sister, a little bossy, but not always on my side when I did things wrong. When I broke her..." And here I think a light went on in Jake's eyes. "I broke her music box. I didn't mean to. It slipped. But then she patted me on the head and said not to worry. I should have known. She loved that music box. It was the only music in the house except if we sang or hummed ourselves. I thought she would kill me so I hid the pieces but not very well, and she found it. And then she..." Jake opened his eyes and took a deep breath, "...she patted me. I was so relieved that I didn't see what was happening. Alyssa would never have let me off the hook. She'd have kept me there wiggling as long as she could and then gone to mother...or I don't know what. I'd still be working it off somehow—her chores or her cleaning or something."

Arbuckle's train of thought came running back to the present. He listened to Jake and recalculated. If I was not Jake's sister, that was still the kind of displacement that could foul the world and plunge the kingdom into... But wait. If the farm girl was not herself, then surely the princess, as he had suspected, was some kind of substitute too. Arbuckle was circling in on the situation having taken the long way around (and his brain may even have stopped for a snack and a drink of water, I think). His "Aha" was glorious as the sunset and startling to animal and insect alike. Jake snorted his approval of the aha and the two heads came together, and plans were hatched just a few feet away from my spying hideout in the loft.

Chapter Nine

I continued my campaign to get the farmers to stop drinking the water, but the belief was too strong: if the water was clear, it was good. If water didn't smell bad, and you could see the clarity, it was good. And their water seemed to flow from the vicinity of the castle pure and odorless. No monsters in the water because monsters could not be that small—unseeable, untasteable, unsmellable. Everyone knew that anything monstrous enough to make everyone sick and even kill some people just had to breathe fire, or thunder down upon them like war or come in the night with great fangs. And the cure would not be fruit and vegetables, that much was clear. A cure for such a great sickness would be that things needed to be put right. Order was everything.

And so the generals, such as they could function, prepared for war (still unclear about whom to attack, but they knew attack they must). The priests and wizards and mages and necromancers burned incense and mixed potions and muttered spells, such as they had the energy for.

Alyssa at the castle kept up her campaign in her own way and also encountered such powerful beliefs and habits and traditions that turning anyone's opinion was like trying to stop a wagon load of wood that was rumbling downhill toward destruction. In court, a pale ghost of court activity was in place. No intrigues but only discussions of bowels and vomit. No ritual but scurrying for the outhouses.

She reported to me that Arbuckle each day moved among the ghosts and ruins of court with a growing certainty that not only was Jake right but that he, Arbuckle Pemberton III, was going to be celebrated in story and song as the savior of the kingdom. His name would ascend to the pantheon of historical kingdom notables, his selfless act resonate among schoolchildren for time immemorial. He felt assured that trumpets would announce his name, hushed whispers of admiration would follow. He paced the court already aglow with his powerful news. He thought about how to stage the telling, how to gather the power of court and blow loud the horn of his news so that everyone would know it was he who had saved the kingdom from two fierce witches and... Were there any dangerous animals involved in the saving act, he wondered? He might add one or two since these unnatural things usually involved some kind of dangerous beast. A battle? Well, not really, but a capture, of course, when the time came. The capturing could present some dangers too. Though they looked like two mere girls, there was no telling what hideous ogres had wrapped themselves in the disguise of innocent girls.

It was Alyssa, of course, telling me what she thought Arbuckle was imagining. I think Alyssa loved filling in, maybe better than he could himself, what Arbuckle was thinking.

He studied the princess who, of course, was a not-princess. He couldn't just up and accuse her. She had all the position and status. And besides, she seemed so healthy, as if she alone somehow had escaped the general malaise and sickness. She seemed to have made a pact with some supernatural force to be spared. He must be careful of whatever that force was. She was on top for the moment—for now, had all the power. For now! He must proceed carefully.

For her part, Alyssa embraced her task. She knew the hill she had to climb to enlighten those who refused the light itself. She would demonstrate the sickening power of the water.

She said she set up two cages as if she were doing the most natural activity in the world for a princess. In one cage she fed three mice only fruit and vegetables, mice she herself had caught in the fields near the castle. And in the other cage, three other mice who had water to drink as well as food. She kept them in the hallway, and each day she wrote down her observations. She spoke to no one about the two cages, explained to no one what she was doing, included no one in her plans.

Arbuckle saw the mice and assumed the worst. The princess-witch now had accomplices in her evil work. Those mice were certainly dangerous far beyond their tiny size and twitching noses.

Arbuckle crept up toward Alyssa, sliding along the castle wall, looking this way and that. He had spied on her outside her lessons regularly, kept his distance, but his shadow always gave him away.

Now she saw his shadow duck down when she called out to him. "Arbuckle. Come here. I have something interesting to show you." She picked up one of the healthy mice and offered it toward where he was hiding. "Look. He won't hurt you. He's very tiny, actually." And then, she told me, she couldn't help herself. Her sense of silly got the best of her. She swallowed down a giggle and kept going. "See. It has a little nose and a little…" But the shadow fled down the long hall, Arbuckle's footsteps gaining speed. She thought he was running as if chased by a wolf. How odd? A tiny mouse would make him fly like that. I wonder what's wrong with him.

Each day the vegetable and fruit eating mice scurried and ate and grew fat. The other cage held tired and listless mice, too sick to mate or romp. They cowered, and one shook constantly. Two died very soon. The remaining one's eyes glazed over, and it lay panting its last hours. The princess went to her experiment more and more obviously, each day sitting at the cages making notes and even trying to chat with those who could still move about the castle.

Finally, one old councilor stopped on his way to respond to his urgent bowels and looked at the mice. "What magic is this you're trying out in the halls, princess?" He had to go, and soon, but the cages and the princess with her pages of notes held him in thrall. "Why do you keep dead mice in a cage?" he croaked. "What have you done to kill them?"

"I gave them water," she said matter-of-factly. "Water. And these"—she indicated the lively cage—"these got no water. I believe the water disagrees with these mice." The last live mouse in the cage rolled on its side, as if on cue, and lay panting into the straw. And then expired.

"Well, that's the last one," she said. "It outlived the others by two days. Here"—and she held up her sheaf of notes—"see how the activity decreases each day and the thirst for more water increased. As if they were trying to kill themselves with the water..."

"Got to go," the old councilor barked, and he was off down the hall. But Alyssa knew he had seen what was necessary. On the other hand, Arbuckle was nowhere to be seen and hadn't even crept around since fleeing into the shadows.

What the councilor had seen was still with him the next day. And the next. He must have felt like a mouse, and he wanted to exchange cages with the healthy mice. He began, on his own, to find ways to avoid the water. The next day he felt a little stronger. The next even better. He had learned quickly. He then persuaded one more convert among the old councilors, and the two of them rose toward health. Word spread. Then a decree: don't drink water until the King says you can.

The priests and other wizards claimed success.

The chanting and smoke and bells and potions and enchantments had worked, they exclaimed.

Those who had read the chicken guts and other critters claimed that *they* had seen the change coming and pointed out their clever prophecy in the coded messages they had announced.

The Alyssa released her live mice and buried her dead mice and slapped her hands together—job done. And smiled. She had managed to teach the old unteachables something true and valuable to the community. She didn't have to have credit for it, so she said nothing as every group in the castle claimed to have solved the problem of sickness. "Water, it was the water!" they all proudly proclaimed. Alyssa smiled. War was called off.

But while the kingdom was getting well, and while the word was sent out to the farms and villages, Arbuckle saw his chances for immortality slipping away, brought low by six mice. He had to strike and quickly before the entire population of court got well. He panicked.

You may have figured out that Arbuckle, who was not stupid, as I said, was also not the sharpest sword in the armory. But he was ambitious, and he was greedy—an unfortunate, but, alas, common combination.

Alyssa acted out for me her very funny version of what was going on in his panicked mind.

He had decided to risk everything and accuse the princess of not being the princess, and also accuse her of being the real reason why the kingdom grew dim with bad water. Alyssa, paced back and forth for me doing her best Arbuckle imitation. And while he was at it, he'd accuse the princess of unnatural acts to bring off her evil plans. And also of enchanting animals. Of being a witch. And he'd.... Wait a minute, he thought. I better be right or I'm dead meat, dead mice, dead or in exile. Exile! Not that. She threw the back of her hand onto her forehead and wailed like an overwrought Arbuckle.

"They'd send me away to live in a...yuk...village. A farm. I'd work all day and cry all night. I'd have to eat dirty food and drink out of wooden cups. I'd have to sleep on the floor with...mice!" Ahhh, she sighed long and sonorous. "I'd better think about this some more. How could Jake help me? How could I make it look like it was his idea if my accusations came back to bite me? Oh, this doesn't feel good." She pranced a little dance like Arbuckle did when he got very excited. "I have to go slow. But by then the kingdom will heal, and I'll have no glory at all. I'll be a cipher the rest of my days. A public fool. A nobody. Go slow. Go fast. Go slow."

Alyssa reported this to me. She very much enjoyed acting out Arbuckle thinking and prancing back and forth like a player on a stage. I laughed and laughed like any appreciative audience.

In the village, I had made converts to my fruit and vegetable diet, but the bad water remained, and no one would do anything about it until some authority sent word. But then word did come trickling down from the castle from councilor to courtier to soldier and kitchen maid and stable hand—it was the water! All the authorities, of course, had claimed wisdom for themselves, and the Alyssa returned to her duties fully expecting the others running the kingdom to fix the water situation. But what to do about the water, they all asked? What can we do about the secret sickness growing there?

And so Alyssa and I decided to risk everything. Jake and Arbuckle (at Arbuckle's urging) did too. Now that everyone was feeling much better, people were out and about in the land, so any of our meetings could be discovered

It was inevitable, I suppose, that the four of us should

somehow collide like planets hurling through the peculiar spaces of the kingdom. Arbuckle in disguise, Alyssa skulking toward the farm in the twilight, I making up excuses to mend a fence and clear a bramble patch after supper, and Jake, as usual, brachiating from tree to tree—all of us came together.

Jake, from his tree, spied us all. Alyssa came over a rise, and there was Arbuckle. I slunk out of a copse, and there were the other two, wide-eyed and stuttering their what-the-hell-you-doing-heres. And Jake with a whoop and a yahoo swung down from his tree and landed perfectly among us.

After the initial denials, the layers of deception dropped away on all four sides.

"And just as I suspected," Arbuckle croaked. "You two are not you two at all."

We looked at each other; was the jig up? Or should we soldier on through and insist on a new lie on top of the old lie? What would you do?

Well, Jake, from the tree-wisdom there at the bottom of his brain, asked the most important question. "What's the difference?" And the rest of us looked at each other, each asking him or her self, yeah, what *is* the difference?

Jake's question hung in the air between us as if a butterfly of truth suddenly riveted our attention. Arbuckle sighed, a sign that he was thinking. Alyssa scratched her nose and pursed her lips. More thinking. Jake began whistling to himself and glancing around to see, I supposed, if there was some high place to swing away. This would have to count for thinking. And I, without much thinking at all, immediately saw that we could do this. There was no difference who did it in what combination or even who got credit for it.

We, after some few words of agreement, decided that all

four of us, were the real difference. That is, we could make the difference that would change the kingdom forever after.

"We are the difference," I announced, hoping to get some kind of cheer going. But Alyssa just laughed. Arbuckle was already rubbing his chin with exaggerated seriousness. And Jake swung away with tree-full grace.

Arbuckle found a way to save himself. Alyssa and I found a way to keep up our very happy switched lives. And Jake, Jake the one who had cut through all the potential confusion and difficulties and phantom impossibilities, Jake the natural philosopher and tree-swinger, he had become heroic without it even occurring to him—the best kind of hero, it turns out.

And so we did our work.

Arbuckle became minister of water (thereby joining his illustrious family with his portrait in the royal galley). He returned to court and led the task of moving the unfortunate dump and protecting the precious water both above and under ground for all time. His motto became, "The water is the gift." And the kingdom had learned what dangers lay very close by if ever their watchfulness waned again. THE GIFT must always be protected, it was proclaimed everywhere.

A banner was sewn with gold thread and decorated with flying, colorful birds on a background of forest green in case anyone might forget, and it said simply, THE GIFT, and was hung across the castle gate. Arbuckle turned his tailor to producing a wardrobe for him of muted green, teal, sage and ecru as he went about his duties as protector of health, guardian of THE GIFT. He stepped into the landscape and blended in only to appear at council meetings as if by some forest magic. And then back to nature, ever vigilant, he swept. It turned out Arbuckle's real talent lay in making up slogans, and THE GIFT caught on and spread to our neighbors. Our kingdom's whole sad tale of bad water, of bad sickness, of tending the land, spread to others, so that we became the lesson they could teach themselves without going through all of our wretchedness.

Alyssa and I at first thought we would have to change what we had been doing. We would have to work our way back to our original lives though neither of wanted to. But Jake's tree-wisdom prevailed. Who was to know about the exchange if none of the four of us revealed it? Arbuckle's theory of things out of place quickly gave way to his rising status at court. Jake kind of liked me, his new sister (and maybe even a little better than the real one; I never told Alyssa that, either). And my passion for the garden dirt, the labor of love on the farm, these were so strong in me that the kingdom could go on primping without my participation. Alyssa had developed a knack for that court business, and the kingdom was better off with her in the princess finery. I gave that up gladly, and she gladly said yes to it all. Finally, the entire court had realized what her mice in the hallway were all about. And she began to show others what great things we could learn by looking carefully at mice—and birds, and insects, rocks, trees, wind, deer, and even under the smallest pebbles in the smallest streams.

And one more thing, it was reported—though it's hard to be certain these days though the witnesses were said to be many—one day there was heard a great and thorough sigh of thanks from somewhere under the earth, somewhere in the wrinkles and cracks and fissures of the land, that the kingdom had turned its eye and heart to keeping the water clean and pure. The witnesses said it was like the great shoulders of the world shrugged and then relaxed.

And joy was in the water—the gift.

Our Street Books

JUVENILE FICTION, NON-FICTION, PARENTING

Our Street Books are for children of all ages, delivering a potent mix of fantastic, rip-roaring adventure and fantasy stories to excite the imagination; spiritual fiction to help the mind and the heart; humorous stories to make the funny bone grow; historical tales to evolve interest; and all manner of subjects that stretch imagination, grab attention, inform, inspire and keep the pages turning. Our subjects include Non-fiction and Fiction, Fantasy and Science Fiction, Religious, Spiritual, Historical, Adventure, Social Issues, Humour, Folk Tales and more.

If you have enjoyed this book, why not tell other readers by posting a review on your preferred book site. Recent bestsellers from Our Street Books are:

Relax Kids: Aladdin's Magic Carpet

Marneta Viegas

Let Snow White, the Wizard of Oz and other fairytale characters show you and your child how to meditate and relax. Meditations for young children aged 5 and up.

Paperback: 978-1-78279-869-9 Hardcover: 978-1-90381-666-0

Wonderful Earth

An interactive book for hours of fun learning

Mick Inkpen, Nick Butterworth

An interactive Creation story: Lift the flap, turn the wheel, look in the mirror, and more.

Hardcover: 978-1-84694-314-0

Boring Bible: Super Son Series 1
Andy Robb
Find out about angels, sin and the Super Son of God.
Paperback: 978-1-84694-386-7

Relax Kids: How to be Happy
52 positive activities for children
Marneta Viegas
Fun activities to bring the family together.
Paperback: 978-1-78279-162-1

Rise of the Shadow Stealers
The Firebird Chronicles
Daniel Ingram-Brown
Memories are going missing. Can Fletcher and Scoop unearth their own lost history and save the Storyteller's treasure from the shadows?
Paperback: 978-1-78099-694-3 ebook: 978-1-78099-693-6

Readers of ebooks can buy or view any of these bestsellers by clicking on the live link in the title. Most titles are published in paperback and as an ebook. Paperbacks are available in traditional bookshops. Both print and ebook formats are available online.

Find more titles and sign up to our readers' newsletter at http://www.johnhuntpublishing.com/children-and-young-adult
Follow us on Facebook at
https://www.facebook.com/JHPChildren
and Twitter at https://twitter.com/JHPChildren